The
Shadowed
Unicorn

The Shadowed Unicorn

Sheila Kelly Welch

Front Street / Cricket Books
Chicago

Library of Congress Cataloging-in-Publication Data
Welch, Sheila Kelly.
The shadowed unicorn/Sheila Kelly Welch.—1st ed.
p. cm.
Summary: When their father dies suddenly, twelve-year-old twins Brendan and
Nick, along with their mother and older sister Ami, move to an isolated old farm
in the country, where the twins find themselves pulled into Ami's obsession with
capturing a unicorn.
ISBN 0-8126-2895-0
[1. Grief—Fiction. 2. Country life—Pennsylvania—Fiction. 3. Twins—Fiction.
4. Brothers and sisters—Fiction. 5. Unicorns—Fiction. 6. Pennsylvania—Fiction.]
I. Title.

PZ7. W44894 Sh 2000
[Fic]—dc21
                                                                99-058253

*To Eloise with love and thanks for all the
years of enthusiastic support*

The
Shadowed
Unicorn

Chapter One

"Get over, Shag. Move!" Nick gave the dog a determined shove.

Shag stumbled over the suitcase on the car seat and landed on Brendan. He shifted his legs, attempting to avoid her sharp toenails. "Can't you stay on the floor?" Brendan asked. Ignoring him, Shag thrust her wet nose into the narrow opening at the top of the window. Long, blond hair drifted off her body. "Sit!" he commanded.

Shag swiveled her head toward Brendan with an anxious gulp. Gobs of sticky dog saliva made spots on his jeans. Some landed on his hot, bare arms, and he half expected it to sizzle. Glancing across the seat at Nick, he saw the way he himself felt—sweaty and exhausted. We're never going to get there, he thought.

Three hours ago, they'd left New York City to drive to their new home, a small farm in Pennsylvania. Just three hours. It felt more like thirty, what with getting lost twice and having to put up with Ami, their fourteen-year-old sister. But no one was asking Mom,

"How much farther?" The back of their mother's head looked tense; she hated to drive.

Brendan looked up into the rearview mirror and saw the reflection of the top portion of Mom's face. Her glasses were smudged and her eyes bloodshot. With one slightly trembling hand, she poked wisps of dark hair behind her ears. He watched silently. He knew that she was doing her best to make life seem normal, even though they all knew that it wasn't.

If Dad hadn't died, he'd have been the one driving, Mom in the passenger seat beside him. And Ami would have been in the backseat, making it even hotter and nastier. But Brendan would have traded years of discomfort to have Dad alive.

"What's that awful smell?" Mom asked abruptly.

"The usual," said Nick. "Shag farted."

Mom said, "Watch your mouth." Brendan knew the odor was coming from Nick's dirty socks, which lay on the floor along with his sneakers, candy wrappers, several soda cans, worn-out batteries for boring games, and tufts of Shag's fur.

"My feet were burning up," Nick whispered defensively. Then he raised his voice so their mother could hear above the roar of a truck. "I'm suffocating. Can't we open these idiot windows some more? We won't let Shag jump out. We promise. We're gonna die without any breeze!"

"Shut up!" Ami's voice cut into the thick air like a dull blade.

Nick jammed his fist into the back of Ami's seat,

and she jerked forward with a curse. The old tiger-striped cat, Shere Khan, gave a raspy mew from her lap.

"Aren't we sweet today," said Nick sarcastically.

"I'm going to toss Khan back there if you don't shut your fat mouth!" Ami lifted the cat toward the ceiling. His cry came out as a squeak, and he scrabbled at the air with his skinny legs.

"Enough!" Mom yelled. Ami dropped the cat back into her lap.

Brendan stared at his brother. *We're gonna die?* he mouthed. Ever since Dad's death shortly before Christmas, they'd avoided phrases like that. Nick shrugged and rolled his eyes.

"We'll be there in about an hour," Mom said, her voice grim. "I hope. And I promise to look into having the air conditioning fixed as soon as I can. Then we won't bake in the car every time we go anywhere the rest of the summer."

Brendan shifted his gaze to watch the highway that was following the dips and rolls of the land. The bright haze made him squint, and his eyelids felt heavy. He yawned and looked again at Nick, who seemed to be falling asleep with his head slumped at an ungainly angle against the window.

Shag whined and climbed into Brendan's lap. He yanked the tail of his T-shirt out from under her rear end and mopped the sweat from his forehead. Yuck! Dog hair! He pushed her, and she slid to the floor with a groan. His legs were numb and sticky, and he needed a bathroom—soon.

With Shag jammed into the narrow space on the floor, there was no room for his feet. "Hey, Ami, you want to trade animals?" he asked. Her answer was a muttered curse.

"Mom, Ami's swearing. Again!" Nick said, his eyes still closed.

"Nick, I don't want to hear it," Mom said.

"What don't you want to hear? Ami swearing or me telling you she's swearing. How come you let *her* get away with it, but not us?"

"Just try to get along for a little while so I can concentrate on driving. Please, you guys!"

"Guys and *gal*," muttered Nick.

Brendan wished he'd never said anything about trading. He stared at Ami's thick, blond hair, pulled back and fastened with a ponytail holder decorated with a plastic ladybug. It looked like something she'd worn years ago. Maybe it was part of her new country image. Yeah, right, he thought. Ami could sure use a new image.

"Can you read that sign, Brendan?" asked Mom. "I'm looking for Route 44. I hope I haven't missed it."

"There it is." Brendan pointed, leaning as far forward as his seat belt would allow.

The exit ramp sloped and curved. Shag scrambled back onto Brendan's lap to get a better view. They traveled a few more miles along a narrow road until they came to a group of buildings. An official-looking sign read "Fernville." Brendan counted eight houses, two churches, a bar, and a gas station.

Nick licked his lips with a smacking sound and said, "I'm hungry."

"You can get a bite while I'm buying gas," Mom said. "Brendan, please walk Shag and give her a drink. Ami, are you getting out?"

Brendan heard his sister's sullen reply, "I'm not at all hungry, Mom," as he staggered out of the car with Shag. After untangling the leash, he let the dog drag him across the hot asphalt to a patch of weeds next to a utility pole. She shoved her nose into an empty potato chip bag. It made a thin, scraping sound as it scurried away from her.

"This is a pee break, Shag, not time to feed your face. Hurry up. I gotta go, too."

The dog lifted her head and stared across the road at the woods. Her tail began to wave, and she strained at the leash. Brendan hopped from one foot to the other.

"Ah, forget it. Come on!" He dragged her back to the car.

The rest room was located at the side of the building. It smelled like stale pee and cigarette smoke. Brendan wet his arms, splashing the water all the way up to the edges of his T-shirt sleeves. There were no paper towels, but he didn't care. Wet arms felt great. He took a gulp of fresh air as he went outside, then entered the gas station in search of a soda machine.

A teenage girl was sitting on a stool behind the glass counter. Brendan selected a drink from a rusty vending machine, but when he pressed the button, there was just the clink of coins.

"It ain't workin'," the girl said gruffly. Brendan jumped, and his hand dropped to his side.

"I told ya before," she said. "It's out of order. I gotta tell ya ten times?"

He glanced toward her, ready to protest, but then he shrugged and half backed out the door and into the wash of heat and sun. That's what happens when we wear look-alike T-shirts, he thought. He saw no point in explaining to the girl that she'd told Nick, his identical twin, about the broken machine. Strangers could never tell them apart. Friends and relatives knew that Nick liked to talk, and they'd say, "Oh, you're Nick," after a few minutes of his chatter. And then, almost as an afterthought, they would add, "So you must be Brendan." Many people just called them "the twins." Even Dad had used "Twins" as if it were their shared name. Like they were joined at the hip. It never seemed to bother Nick, and when he was younger, Brendan hadn't cared either. But the past couple of years, it had made him feel uncomfortable. He wasn't sure why.

Brendan squeezed into the car, trying unsuccessfully to avoid Shag's welcoming licks. "Why didn't you tell me the soda machine's broken?" he asked Nick. "I lost seventy-five cents."

"So you had an encounter with the teenage witch, too. A real charmer. Puberty does that to some people." Nick paused a moment to stare at the back of Ami's head, but when she didn't react, he shoved the chewed-on end of his candy bar toward Brendan's mouth. "Here, have some."

"No way. That'd just make me more thirsty. Hey,

Ami, is there any of that fruit punch left in the thermos up there?" But Ami completely ignored his question. In a moment, their mother returned and started the car.

Brendan held one arm out stiffly to ward off Shag. He squeezed his eyes shut, determined to follow Nick's example and sleep away the miles.

We're never going to get there, he thought again as he plucked a dog hair off his tongue.

Chapter Two

"This animal's going into a major frenzy," Nick said. As the car slowed, Shag had begun to scramble and pant.

"We're almost there," Mom said. "Now, if we pass a giant oak tree on the left . . . Ah, there! Just as I remembered." She swung the car into an opening between trees with huge trunks.

Brendan looked ahead and saw a driveway that could be more accurately described as a path. It consisted of two ruts with a humped-up, overgrown strip of grassy soil between them. He could hear the swish of grass and weeds against the underside of the car.

"Oh, Lord. I hope we don't gouge out something important," their mother said, peering anxiously out her side window and slowing down even more.

"*This* is it?" Nick leaned forward to stare around Ami's shoulder.

"Get back," she said angrily, snapping her fingers in his face.

Nick swatted her head, and Ami grabbed for his hand but missed.

10

"Stop it!" Mom said.

Nick made a face, slid back onto his seat, and pulled on his crusty socks.

The trees formed a wall on either side of the car, and the leaves on the intertwining branches were a green roof above.

"I've got my sneakers on," Nick announced with a grin. "Nicholas Rodrick, ready for anything. Hey, Mom, we could walk the rest of the way. Then the car wouldn't ride so low."

"Good idea. Take Shag. And watch that Khan doesn't leap out when you open the door. Ami, hang onto him." Brendan could see that Ami had folded her arms and was not making any attempt to restrain the old cat. "I knew we should have bought a cat carrier," Mom said with a weary sigh. "Anyhow, I think this lane—or whatever—is about a mile long." She stopped the car and reached over to put a hand on Khan.

Brendan wrapped the leash around his fist, flung open the car door, then clung desperately as Shag exploded into freedom. She plunged for the underbrush at the edge of the lane, snuffling the country odors. "Don't let go of her!" Mom yelled. "And, boys, don't follow the car too closely."

"O.K., O.K.!" Nick slammed the door shut and waved one hand in dismissal. Their mother accelerated slowly. The car crept away, its undercarriage still dragging through the weeds.

The smell of exhaust blended with the scent of unfamiliar vegetation. Trunks and leaves surrounded them, blocking out the sun. The air felt chilly compared to the temperature in the sweltering car. Brendan hadn't been sure about this move, and now—as he rotated his arm to assess the damage done by Shag's pulling—he felt a prickle of apprehension. Or was he sensing the possibility of adventure? He squinted at the many shades of green. "We're in an emerald tunnel," he told Nick.

"And we're following the Yellow Brick Road." Nick pointed to the gravel lane. Birds chirped beyond the barrier of brush and tree trunks. "It's like . . . like we've slipped back in time or something. Or gone to, like, Oz or someplace."

They walked slowly, allowing the car to disappear around a curve. Nick said, "I hope we don't have to trek this whole way to catch some hillbilly school bus this fall."

Brendan shrugged. School was too far off to worry about now.

It took them over a quarter of an hour to reach the end of the woods. They both stopped and looked out across the clearing, seeing their new home for the first time. The house was partially hidden by clusters of overgrown bushes. Next to the barn on the left was an area enclosed with a sturdy-looking fence.

"Guess what." Nick glared at the unmown yard. "We're going to be lawn boys."

"Come here, you two slowpokes," their mother called. She had parked by the path that led to the front door and had already unloaded the contents of the car onto the grass. The cooler, suitcases, a small bag of kitty litter and a pan, and several cardboard boxes lay in a jumble. Ami was still in the front seat, her right hand draped over the cat's back in a halfhearted effort to prevent him from escaping. Mom's voice dropped as she leaned over and stuck her head close to Ami's window. "O.K., you can get out now. Get a grip on Khan. He'll be scared and want to take off."

Ami was shoving open the door as the boys drew alongside. She climbed out slowly, the cat cradled in one arm. There was something about her movements that reminded Brendan of a person walking through water, as if she were partially submerged.

"Hey, Ami," Nick said loudly. "Isn't this place perfect? Look at all that grass and space and stuff. Even a fence. Room for three horses."

She scowled at him silently. Their mother said, "Here, let me have the cat. You've hardly got a grip on him."

"Whatever," Ami mumbled.

"Be careful, Ami, please! Don't drop him!" There was a ragged edge to Mom's words. Shag gave Shere Khan a friendly sniff during the clumsy transfer to Mom's arms.

The path leading to the house was made of gray stones that were nearly hidden by encroaching crab grass. The house was built of the same kind of stones, and Brendan thought it looked solid. Each of its windows was bracketed by dark blue, peeling shutters.

As they all trooped onto the narrow front porch, the wooden planks sagged. Brendan walked on his heels, wondering if his whole leg or just his foot would go through if a board broke. He noticed that Ami had

13

picked up one of the boxes from the pile next to the car and was now clutching it in her skinny arms. It was labeled "Ami's Stuff. Keep Out! This means you!"

"The place looks different," said Mom uncertainly. "I guess twenty years can cause changes. No, it's more like thirty."

"Thirty years of neglect," muttered Nick, poking one finger at the shaggy paint on a porch post. Mom didn't seem to hear as she fumbled the key into the lock with one hand while holding Khan firmly with the other.

The door opened on creaky hinges, and Mom disappeared into the gloom. Ami pushed roughly past the boys. "It's dark," she said accusingly.

Brendan followed with Shag close on his heels. He slid his hand along the wall and flicked a switch. The overhead light came to life, revealing an ornate fixture dotted with dead flies. They were in a large, empty living room with six windows shrouded in heavy drapes. A fireplace built into one wall still held a pile of ashes and a few charred sticks of wood.

"Let me open these," said their mother, pulling one of the cords. The drapes moved back with a sigh and a cascade of dust. A pervasive odor of musty, closed-in air made Brendan wrinkle his nose.

"Disgusting," muttered Ami, sneezing and hiding her face behind her box.

Nick shut the door, and their mother plopped Shere Khan onto the floor. The cat stood still, only the tip of his tail flicking back and forth. After a moment, he walked cautiously across the room and down the hallway.

Shag pulled at the end of her leash, so Brendan let go of it. The dog careened around the living room, checking out each corner with loud sniffs. The leash made swirling trails on the dusty floor.

Brendan followed Shere Khan and discovered a large kitchen with dark, greasy-looking cabinets and a nicked enamel sink. The cat climbed onto a countertop and gave a demanding yowl. "The Return of the Voice—a miracle brought on by the thought of food," said Brendan.

"What a cozy, comfy kitchen," Nick said sarcastically. He came in and began pulling open drawers and peering into cupboards. "It's sure empty."

"It's supposed to be, silly," Mom said as she joined them. "I asked the lawyer to arrange an auction right after we inherited the place."

"They sold the food and everything?" asked Nick, then he added in the rapid voice of an auctioneer, "How much for this quarter-full box of cornflakes? Do I hear one dollar, one dollar, one dollar?"

"Two cents," offered Brendan.

Mom grinned. "Anyhow, I didn't want to arrive and find heaps of junk. The movers will be bringing our things tomorrow. I hope. So we'll have to spend some time cleaning." She ran a finger along the top of the counter and grimaced at the dust.

Ami entered the kitchen, and everyone looked at her. Sunlight coming through the dusty windows above the sink caught the loose strands of hair around her head and bleached them white. She stared at the window, her eyes like expressionless blue marbles. She still held her box in front of her, almost as if it were some sort of shield.

Looking at his sister gave Brendan an uneasy feeling in the pit of his stomach. Ever since their father's death, she'd begun acting spooky. He and Nick called it her zombie act. That made it sound funny, but it wasn't. Brendan reached over and plucked Khan off the counter and pressed him against his chest. The cat began to purr loudly, breaking the silence.

"Well, what do you think of the house, Ami?" asked Mom.

"It's O.K., I guess." She shrugged. "A little . . . uh . . . dirty, isn't it?"

Mom laughed, sounding more relieved than amused. Just then, Khan began to squirm, so Brendan set him down.

"Come on," Nick demanded. "Let's go upstairs and pick out our rooms."

"I forget how many bedrooms there are," their mother said vaguely. She followed the boys back into the short hallway. "The steps are right over here." She motioned toward a door.

They climbed the narrow, twisting staircase single file. Mom said, "Be careful! One time your uncle Michael fell all the way down and was out cold for an hour. I don't want any concussions or broken bones. The nearest hospital is miles away. . . ."

Upstairs they found four bedrooms with low ceilings and windows set so near the floor, they had to crouch to lean their elbows on the sills. The bathroom was tiny and smelled of mold.

16

As they stepped back into the upstairs hallway, Nick said, "We can each have our own room." His gaze shifted quickly to Brendan. "I mean, if we want to." The twins had always shared a room, just as they shared everything.

"Where's mine?" asked Ami, coming up the stairs with Shag scrambling after her.

"Take your pick," said Mom. "But I'd like the one next to the bathroom. If you boys decide to share, we'll have a guest room. If not, we'll put the futon downstairs in what's going to be my studio. Visitors who manage to find us can sleep there with my art supplies. It's up to you boys."

"You want to share, or what?" asked Nick.

"I want this one," said Ami.

"But that's the one by the bathroom," Nick said, letting the annoyance show in his voice. Ami ignored him as she carried her box into the room.

Brendan glanced at their mother, but she just sighed, then shrugged. "It's O.K. Ami can have it." Mom poked her head in the door. "Yellow, a cheerful color. I'll take the beige room."

"That leaves us a choice of dirty purple or puke green." Brendan stuck out his tongue.

"I've got the stronger stomach," said Nick. "I'll take the green one."

So he's decided we aren't going to share, Brendan thought.

"Don't worry, boys," said Mom. "I plan to buy paint so you can redo your walls."

Brendan wasn't worried about paint. He went into

his room alone and looked around. The purple walls *were* dirty, and the plaster was uneven, almost lumpy in places. He tested the door; its hinges squeaked. On the inside of the door was a mirror.

He sat on the floor next to one of the three windows, and Shag trotted over and leaned against his side. Brendan unsnapped her leash, then wrapped one arm around her neck and scratched behind her ears. She stared out the window with him.

They didn't move even when the others went downstairs.

Chapter Three

Later that afternoon, Mom drove them to a store located only five minutes from the farm. The store was actually the first floor of a house that stood next to a narrow road. A sign, suspended over the entrance to the road, read "Magnolia Acres" in red paint, faded to dusty pink. Brendan counted thirty-one mailboxes on a long, sagging board supported by three posts.

"The trailer court," Mom explained, pointing at the sign. "It was here even when I was a kid. But the store is new to me." She pushed her hair off her forehead. There were purplish smudges under her eyes and a streak of dirt on one cheek. No one told her.

"I have to make a couple of calls," Mom said, heading toward an outside pay phone.

The children walked into the store, past the plump, bland-faced woman at the cash register. Brendan was sure she was watching them with her watery eyes and thinking about twins. Why did people always act as if twins were some sort of freaks?

Ami stopped and frowned at the list Mom had written on a scrap of paper. Nick reached for it. "Here, give it to me," he said.

"Mom gave it to me, stupid," said Ami. "Get your dirty paws away from me." She held the list above her head as if daring him to jump up and grab it.

Nick shrugged. "Fine, Little Miss Sweet Mouth. We'll just get the Popsicles."

"No, you two boys get all the food stuff." Ami neatly ripped off the bottom of the list and shoved it at Brendan. He felt like making her eat it, but that would have required a real struggle, and this was, after all, a public place. List in his hand, Brendan wandered up and down the narrow aisles with Nick until they had collected everything except the Popsicles.

"What kind do you want?" asked Nick, leaning into the low freezer along the back wall.

Brendan moved closer to the freezer, and the cool air raised goose bumps on his arms. "Any kind. How about a package with lots of flavors?"

Before Nick could answer, they heard a high-pitched giggle. From behind a rack of mops, a little girl was peeking at them. She grinned. Her front teeth looked too big for her mouth. She hid them behind her cupped hand as another giggle escaped.

"It's us," muttered Nick. "You know, the twin bit. She thinks we're some kind of weirdos. I'll fix her." He thrust his head forward, widened his eyes into a crazed stare, and growled fiercely.

With a squeal of mock terror, the girl leaped away, knocking three mops onto the floor with a clatter. She scuttled off and disappeared down an aisle.

"Mad Dog Nick hasn't lost his touch," Nick said, helping Brendan replace the mops. One hung precariously, and Brendan kept glancing at it, wondering when it would fall, but Nick went back to rummaging through the boxes of Popsicles. "I can't find any banana flavor," he complained.

"Ami hates banana," Brendan said.

"I know." Nick smiled. "Serve her right if we get something she hates. She's such a pain!"

They heard a scuffling sound behind them and then an annoyed whisper. "Sandy, stop it." Turning, they saw a boy about their own age pulling the girl toward the freezer case. She was yanking back, bracing her sneakered feet against the linoleum until her soles skidded and squeaked. The boy shook his head in exasperation. "Stop acting like a baby. You've seen twins before."

"No, Jonny, not boys this big," said Sandy, twisting free of her brother's grasp. "Just the Warren twins in third grade. And they're girls."

The boy shrugged, then grinned at Nick and Brendan. "Sorry. She's only seven."

Sandy stared at Nick. "He's the one that growled. I think."

Nick said, "Nah, it was him." He nodded toward Brendan. "Down, Fido."

Sandy looked at Brendan, wrinkling her brow in concentration. She shook her head and turned back to Nick. "It was you." Then she added, "How come I never seen you guys before?"

"We just came. We're moving here," said Nick.

"Yeah? Where? In town?" asked Jonny.

"Nah. To some old place out in the country."

Brendan saw Ami approaching the checkout. He reached into the freezer and grabbed a box of multi-flavored Popsicles. "Come on, Nick. We gotta go. Ami's done, and she's got the money."

"See ya 'round," said Nick to the boy. He gave one more growl in Sandy's direction.

She giggled, then pointed toward a teenage boy. "That's my biggest brother, Greg. He's sixteen and a half. I bet he could beat you up."

"Thanks for sharing that," said Nick. "Think he'll beat me up if I get in line ahead of him?"

"Sure!"

"Jeez, Sandy, give it a rest," said Jonny. "So long, you guys."

Brendan wanted to leave quickly and quietly, but it took forever to get through the checkout. Ami had a whole pile of cleaning items their mother had requested. The cashier worked slowly, glancing up often and smiling at them. Brendan was sure she was searching unsuccessfully for differences between him and Nick. Ami fumbled with the money, dropping some coins on the counter in the process of paying.

Nick gave a disgusted snort, grabbed a bag, and headed for the door. As Brendan picked up another load, he saw Sandy wave. She probably thinks I'm Nick, he thought. Then he noticed that Sandy's oldest brother was watching Ami with interest, a faint smile on his face.

As they walked out, Brendan heard the distinctive clank of a mop falling to the floor.

• • •

That night at supper, Nick announced, "I'm going to paint a mural in my room."

They were all sitting on the back steps, eating bologna sandwiches on white bread with no mayonnaise because they'd forgotten to buy any. Brendan stared at the tall grass that should have been the backyard. Their mother had told them not to sit out there. "Ticks," she'd said ominously.

"My mural will be perfect," continued Nick. He never cared if anyone was listening. "I'm going to have these little hands reaching up all around. On the wall. Only way down low near the floor. Like there're these people trapped underneath, trying to escape."

Mom shook her head, but she looked amused.

"Revolting," said Ami. She got up and slouched back into the house, letting the flimsy screen door clap shut behind her.

Nick nodded. "Revolting is a good word. Macabre is better. Then when we make some friends around here, we'll invite them over and scare the you-know-what out of them. By the way, we met a kid at the store today."

"Oh, really? What's his name?" Mom sounded truly interested.

"Don't remember. Something like Sammy, I think."

"No," said Brendan. "Sandy. But that wasn't the boy, that was his little sister. His name's Jonny. And Greg's the older one. The big brother."

"I'm glad you're making friends already," said Mom. "So, were these kids you met nice?"

Brendan gagged down another soggy lump of sandwich.

"Nice?" Nick shrugged. "Didn't you see them? Oh yeah. You weren't in the store. Who cares about nice, anyhow. The oldest one could bench 275, right, Brendan? You think? Big muscles. He sure looked Ami over good."

"Well," their mother said, "Ami's a very attractive girl."

Yeah, right. Brendan was sure their mother would not have approved of Greg's intense stare. He stood up and wadded his napkin in his fist. "Look," he said, pointing out across the yard and the meadow beyond. A bank of thick, gray clouds was moving over the tops of the hills. Lightning shimmered at its edges, and a chill breeze lifted the hair off his forehead.

"Get inside, boys." Mom sounded apprehensive. "That storm'll be here soon."

They had just entered the kitchen when they heard a shriek from Ami. She tore down the hallway from the living room, flapping her hands frantically above her head and screaming, "Bat! Bat! Get it away from me!" Without stopping, she scrambled up the stairs, slamming the door hard behind her.

Nick's mouth hung open. "A bat in the house?" He and Brendan followed Mom cautiously into the living room. All of them ducked as the small, brown creature swooped over their heads. Shere Khan was standing in the middle of the floor, his head tipped back, his gaze following the bat's flight with total concentration.

At last the bat landed on the bricks above the

mantel and clung there as if hoping to become invisible. Shere Khan stalked across the room toward it.

"Good grief! I had no idea Khan had such a killer instinct," Mom said as she scooped him up into her arms. "That poor bat must have come down the chimney." Brendan went to the mantel for a closer look. The bat's leathery wings were surprisingly fragile, and its tiny body expanded and contracted with each breath. "Don't touch it!" Mom warned. "It could have rabies."

Following their mother's instructions, Nick and Brendan were able to capture the bat under a cup, slip a piece of cardboard beneath it, and take the makeshift trap outside. Brendan slid off the cardboard, and the bat scrambled out to fly away. In just a few seconds, it looked like a scrap of black paper being blown helter-skelter before the approaching clouds. Brendan blinked, and it was gone.

When they got back inside the house, Nick yelled up the stairs at Ami, "You can come out of hiding now, Miss Scaredy-Cat. Your brave brothers saved you from the rabid vampire bat."

"Shut up!" came her muffled retort.

Soon premature darkness arrived with the clouds. Inside the house, it seemed night had fallen. Mom requested that the children mop their bedroom floors, and Brendan discovered that he needed to turn on the overhead light to see. When he was finished, he spread out his sleeping bag on the still-damp floor. It was way too early for bed, but he didn't care.

He took off his sneakers and socks and flung them into a corner. Then, still wearing his clothes, he crawled inside the sleeping bag. It smelled of smoky bonfires from family camping trips in the Catskills before their father's death. He remembered roasting marshmallows. Ami always let hers burn and twirled around with the miniature torch waving in the darkness. Dad would laugh and threaten to make her eat the charred lump. Ami would scream and then giggle at his teasing. It seemed a long time ago. Now Brendan breathed in through his nose and held the campfire-scented air inside. He lay still, as if listening for another sound, another voice.

"You going to sleep?" Nick asked. He was standing in the doorway, a pail of water in one hand.

"Maybe. I'm tired."

"O.K." Nick left, and Brendan could hear him thumping about in the room next-door.

Thunder grumbled, and Brendan rolled over. The wooden floor was hard and unyielding. He shut his eyes and listened to the storm. Rumbles turned to crashes. Here in the country, there were none of the city street sounds to drown out the noise. The storm was raw and wild. Lightning flashes bounced off the walls, brightening the darkness even behind his closed lids.

A huge crash made his eyes pop open in terror and his heart go into overdrive. The house was totally dark, and he could hear Mom muttering in the bathroom.

"Stay put, you kids," she called. "Just a power failure. It'll be fixed by morning, probably. You all O.K.?"

Brendan and Nick each yelled, "Yeah!" from their bedrooms, but when Ami didn't answer, Brendan heard Mom's halting steps going to her room.

"Ami? You asleep already?" Mom sounded tired. Ami's answer was indistinct, but he heard their mother's slightly sarcastic reply, "Sorry I asked."

A few minutes later, Nick was back at Brendan's doorway. "Hey! I'm coming in." He trailed his sleeping bag across the floor like an oversized security blanket, stepping on Brendan's foot and then flopping down beside him. "Some storm, huh?" he asked. "I bet Ami about peed her pants when that lightning struck so close."

"Yeah."

"Remember that fierce storm the time we were camping, and Ami started crying, and Dad started telling that story. . . ." Nick's voice was cut off by a clap of thunder.

"Sure. I remember," Brendan said when the noise outside had lowered to a grumble. Their dad had always told stories. And he'd read to them, too. Usually fantasies. Just last year Dad and Ami had taken turns reading aloud Tolkien's whole trilogy. But the stories they'd loved best were the ones Dad made up himself. Somehow he always managed to make the children feel as if they were part of the tales. When they'd been younger, Ami had joined the boys in acting out some of the stories.

Now Brendan said, "And remember that time we were camping, and Dad told a story with those two dwarves? And we started pretending to be dwarves . . ."

"And we ran all around the campfire screaming until Mom got mad," finished Nick.

"We could, you know, do that again," said Brendan slowly.

"What? Run around screaming and make Mom mad?"

"No, tell a story. Pretend, the way we used to do with Dad." Brendan watched lightning flicker across the wall of his new room.

"Yeah," Nick said. "We could be these two dwarves, and we get caught by this humongous thunderstorm that the evil wizard has conjured up, and we're in this old castle with lots of bats."

"Right! Bats!" Brendan grinned. "And the castle has a dungeon without end. The Eternal Dungeon. It's filled with vampire bats."

"Yes!" said Nick. "And we're trying desperately to get out of the castle, but one of us is injured and can't move."

"Right. Which one?"

"Me. A dragon got me. In the gut." Nick gagged and groaned.

"O.K. Maybe I've got a healing potion or something."

"No, I've got a better idea. The lightning has powers. It can kill or cure, depending," said Nick.

"Depending on what?" Brendan asked, then said, "I know! If the lightning hits directly, it kills. If it's reflected, it cures."

"Good! I like that. But we gotta have a mirror."

Brendan crawled out of his sleeping bag and groped for the door. He swung it shut just as lightning flashed. In the long mirror attached to the back of the door, for just a fraction of a second, he saw his pale, solitary reflection.

Then Nick yelled, "I'm cured!" and Brendan laughed.

Chapter Four

Sunlight woke Brendan the next morning. It lay on his face like a hot, bright sheet, and he squinted even before opening his eyes. His brother was a large lump inside a bundle of sleeping bag.

Quietly, Brendan got up, being careful not to disturb Shere Khan, who had spent the night curled up at his feet. Brendan went to look out the one window that faced the backyard. When he shoved it open, the rain-washed air felt like a splash of cold water on his face. He peered through the branches of a tree growing next to the small back porch. In the distance was a woodland, rising up and up as if the trees grew taller and taller. It was a hill more like a mountain. The barn was too far off to the side for him to see it, and no other houses were in sight. Brendan felt as if he'd been plunked down in Central Park only to discover that all the surrounding buildings had been vaporized.

He turned from the window to give Nick's sleeping bag a kick. "Wake up. Get outta bed."

"Go away" came the sleep-slurred reply. "Besides, I'm not in bed."

"I'm going outside. Come on. If Mom catches us, she'll tie us to brooms or mops." Brendan sat down and pulled on his shoes.

"O.K. I'll be there," Nick mumbled as he burrowed deeper into his sleeping bag. With a shrug, Brendan left. He made a quick stop in the bathroom. It had an old-fashioned bathtub sitting on claw feet, and the walls were covered with peeling paper that swam with exotic, open-mouthed fish. Bizarre! He looked in the mirror briefly, imitating the fishes' mouths, and thought about brushing his teeth but didn't.

He went carefully down the twisted staircase and was just slipping along the hallway to the back door, when his mother's voice came from the kitchen. "Brendan?"

"Yeah?"

"We're lucky. The power's back on. Come have some breakfast. You're the first one up."

"Not really, Mom." His mother had tied a floral scarf around her head, and she was kneeling on the countertop, a wet sponge in her hand. All the doors to the upper cabinets were wide open.

"You're right. I've been up since six because Shag was whining to go outside. I've tied her by the back door, and she's busy digging a hole next to the porch like a real farm dog. You want some breakfast? We've got cereal or peanut butter and crackers."

Brendan made a face, but his stomach growled hungrily. While he spread peanut butter on crackers, breaking three plastic knives in the process, his mother talked. "The new refrigerator's going to be delivered today. And the phone's hooked up."

He nodded, pointing to his mouth that was almost stuck shut with cracker crumbs and peanut butter. He filled a small paper cup with water and gulped it down, then took another drink. The water had an unfamiliar metallic taste and was so cold it numbed his tongue.

His mother had stopped working. She was perched on the kitchen counter, looking at him, her legs swinging and heels thumping gently into the lower cabinets. "I remember sitting here when I was a little girl."

"Why'd you sit up there?" he asked. "They didn't have chairs?"

She smiled. "I was about five years old, playing out in the pasture, when I tripped and cut my knee on one of those rocks that are everywhere around here. I came in screaming, blood running down my leg. It looked grucsome. So Gramma set me on the counter, right here next to the sink. Then she washed off my knee." Mom nodded toward the center of the room. "I remember that a big table sat right there. It had a bowl of bananas and apples in the middle. Funny. It all seems so clear."

Brendan pulled himself up onto the countertop, too. He crumpled his paper cup and tossed it toward a plastic trash bag draped over a box. He missed.

"I wanted to live here when I was little," Mom went on. "I loved it. But after Gramma and Grandpa died, we only visited a few times. It wasn't the same. I was growing up. Uncle Martin was here alone, and whenever we came, he got all flustered. So we stopped coming. Mother just sent him Christmas cards. Then she got sick. And before the next Christmas, she was gone."

Gone, thought Brendan. Like Dad. He looked down at his feet.

Mom sighed. "I knew my father wouldn't write to Uncle Martin. So I did it for years and years. He never wrote back. For all I knew, he was throwing those cards and notes in the trash unread. I told about things that must have seemed silly, I guess, to an old man. About you kids. Like, 'Ami loves horses and is still taking riding lessons. Sometimes we think she'll turn into a horse. She wants us to call her hair a mane. . . .'" Her voice trailed off. Brendan waited for her to tell what she'd written about him and Nick, but his mother was quiet. He tried to match his feet-swinging to hers.

"Your dad thought I was a little nuts." Mom smiled. "You know, writing to Old Uncle Martin again and again. But I guess I thought he sort of needed to hear from somebody. And then, when we got that letter in September, saying that I'd inherited the farm, your dad was so excited."

Brendan didn't want her to go on. If she kept talking, she would come to the bad part—the day that had changed everything—when a stupid accident left a hole in their family.

"Do you like this place?" Mom looked at him anxiously, as if she could read his thoughts.

"Yeah, Mom." He was relieved that she had changed the subject.

"You think you'll miss your friends in New York a whole lot?"

Brendan shrugged. Missing friends didn't compare to missing Dad, but Mom wasn't talking about that.

"Nah, not too much. You know. Nick and I have each other."

Mom nodded. "And Ami seems a little . . . better? Don't you think? I mean, before the bat episode. She has been helpful, like at the store yesterday. And when I peeked in her room this morning, I saw she had part of her unicorn collection already arranged on her window sill."

"She's fine." Brendan squirmed on the counter. So that's what had been in the box. A bunch of stuffed toys and models Ami had been collecting forever and was too old for now. His sister was a mystery to him. But if it made Mom feel better to think she was improved, so what?

"I think I can afford to buy her a horse," Mom said. "But she hasn't asked for one. Not since . . . December. Now that we're actually here, I think she'll get interested. Again."

"Sure. Maybe." But Brendan was remembering Ami's tantrum when their father had told them about moving to the farm.

"There's no way you'll get me to go there!" she'd screamed. "Don't promise me a horse, Dad. I want a horse here, in New York. I want to stay *here*. *You* go! Go live in the middle of a tick-infested swamp. But *I'm* not going!"

His mother looked at Brendan now and said, "Ami probably regrets the way she reacted to the idea of moving. It was just . . ." She shrugged. "Just bad timing, I guess. I do think living here will be good for her. Better even than seeing that psychologist." Mom chewed her thumbnail thoughtfully and said, "We just have to give Ami time."

Brendan had begun to feel a familiar ache in his throat. His mother's eyes met his, then her gaze slipped away and seemed to fasten on the invisible table from long ago.

"Brendan, I . . ." Her voice had gotten hoarse suddenly. "I talk too much to you. I know it. Sometimes I feel as if you're the listener. The ears."

"And Nick's the mouth, right?" said Brendan lightly.

"What?" called Nick as he clumped down the stairs. "Why didn't you wake me up? What's for breakfast? I'm starving!" He came into the kitchen still chattering. "Some fool opened the window, and there was all this fresh air and sun and screaming birds. Where're the pancakes and sausage and strawberries and cream? This is the *country*, right?"

Brendan handed his brother the jar of peanut butter.

"Oh, puke," said Nick, but he dug his finger in and pulled out a large glob.

"Get out of here," said their mother. "Before you drop that on my clean floor."

"O.K. We're going exploring," said Nick.

"Not too far," Mom said, her brow creased. "You might get lost. The woods go on and on. And that old barn probably has a rotten floor. I don't know, maybe you'd better wait. . . ."

"This is the country. Remember? It's safe," said Nick. "Pure! Healthful! Wholesome!"

"When the movers come with our stuff, we won't be in the way," Brendan added.

Mom sighed. "I'm no match for you two. Not when you join forces. But watch out for poison ivy. It's got three shiny leaves. And remember to stay out of deep brush and grass. Ticks are fierce this time of year. We need to get some repellent."

"Right, Mom," said Nick. He grabbed Brendan's arm and propelled him into the hallway. "Meantime, we'll tell all the ticks to eat the poison ivy."

As they tramped out onto the back porch, they heard her say, "Blood. Ticks suck blood."

"Watch out! Here comes a vampire tick!" Nick pinched the back of Brendan's neck.

Brendan grabbed his brother's wrist and with one quick, expert twist had Nick's arm pinned behind his back. "I'm going to dump you in poison ivy up to your neck! Quick, where is some?"

Shag leaped to greet them but was stopped by her chain. She clawed the air and balanced on her back feet like a frenzied, trained bear, her yelps half strangled by her collar.

"Shut up, will ya?" begged Nick, flapping his free hand at her.

Brendan released Nick's arm. "Poor baby," he said as he hopped off the porch steps and endured Shag's greeting. "You think you're still a puppy."

"Yeah," said Nick. "P.P., remember?"

Brendan nodded as he scratched Shag's head. When they'd gotten her—a tiny scrap of fur with chocolate-drop eyes—she'd made puddles all over the newspaper they'd spread in the kitchen. Their father had started calling her Little P.P., short for Perpetual Pup. She'd

35

gotten house-trained, eventually, but whenever she acted particularly immature, the old nickname resurfaced. No one had used it recently.

"She sure hates being tied up," remarked Nick. "Think we should take her along exploring?"

"Not me. My arm's still sore from yesterday when she dragged me up the driveway."

"And you about broke mine a minute ago," Nick said. "Let's just turn her loose."

Brendan shook his head. "She'd run off."

"So what? She'd come back. I mean what's out there?" Nick nodded toward the expanse of trees and fields.

"Nothing except thousands of little furry things to chase, miles of woods to get lost in, roads to get hit on . . ."

"Ah, quit it. You're starting to sound like Mom. Come on over here, Shaggie. Atta girl." Nick gave the dog a pat, unhooked her chain, and stepped back. Shag cavorted around them.

"Mistake," Brendan said. He tried to grab Shag's collar, but she danced out of reach. Suddenly she stopped, turned away, and lifted her nose to sniff. With one excited yelp, she took off across the overgrown lawn, heading for the field beyond.

Nick whistled for her.

"Fat chance," muttered Brendan.

"Come on. We've got to catch her," said Nick. "I don't want to scream at her, or Mom'll hear."

The dog was only visible in brief snatches as she bounded through the meadow. Nick ran after her, and

Brendan followed, cursing through his teeth as he stumbled through the thick, tall grass. At a small grove of trees, he caught up with Nick.

"She . . . she . . . ," his brother panted. "Ran that way, I think." He pointed toward the woods.

"No point in chasing her. You know that. It never works. Like that time in Central Park." Brendan could still feel the frustration and humiliation of trying to catch Shag that day. Each time they'd gotten within reach, she'd twirled away and dashed off, her mouth gaping as if in silent laughter. She'd only let them catch her when she had gotten tired.

Nick wiped his forehead with the back of his arm. "Yeah. She thinks it's a game."

"Maybe if we just stay here and call her . . ." Brendan whistled and yelled, "Here, Shag!" But there was no answering bark. No fluffy shape hurtling toward them. A bird in the tree above gave an indignant chirp and flapped away.

"How'll I tell Mom?" asked Nick anxiously.

"Don't. Try keeping quiet for a change, bigmouth. Shag's bound to come back soon."

Nick swore and slammed his foot against a tree trunk. He spent the next few moments hopping around clasping his toe. "Ow! Hurts!"

"Right."

"Don't be so sympathetic," Nick said sarcastically. "Besides, you should have stopped me."

"From what? Letting Shag loose? Or kicking the tree?"

"Both. No, just Shag. 'Cause if you'd stopped me

from doing *that,* I wouldn't have done *this.*" Nick sat down on a large stone. His face was flushed, and his eyes had the squinty look they got when he was trying not to cry.

Brendan watched as his brother yanked off his sneaker and wriggled his toes. "Not broken," said Nick. "Should be. Serve me right. Just when Mom's starting to act sort of happy, I go and let her dog get lost."

"Be worse if it was broken," Brendan said. "Mom'd freak out with a trip to the emergency room. Probably not a good hospital for fifty miles. Which would have meant more driving."

"Shut up!" The edge to Nick's voice told Brendan he meant it.

They walked back slowly, trying to follow the faint path of parted grass that had formed when they ran through it. But already the grass had sprung up, obliterating their trail, as if they'd never been there.

Brendan's jeans were soaked with rainwater from the grass. His legs felt heavy, and he could feel a raw scraping where the folds rubbed against the backs of his knees. A large fly dive-bombed against his left ear, and he swatted at it with disgust.

When they reached the backyard, they stopped and exchanged a look, weighing their lost interest in exploring against facing their mother and having her ask about Shag. Neither of them wanted to go back inside.

"Let's check out the barn," suggested Nick.

The exterior of the old building was a combination of weatherworn wood and stone. Deep windows were set along the wall at regular intervals. The boys entered the lower level through a narrow door next to an unwieldy-looking large one. Nick wiped his nose on his sleeve. He spoke in a whisper as he pointed toward the ceiling. "Spooky place. Look at all those spider webs . . . and spiders."

"Charlotte, where are you?" called Brendan.

"So who are you? Wilbur?" asked Nick.

"Right. *Oink! Oink!* Remember when Mom read us *Charlotte's Web?*"

Nick brushed away a cobweb. "Sure. Except for the chapter where Charlotte dies."

Brendan glanced at his brother. Neither one of them said anything for a moment. But he knew that Nick was remembering. Their father had read that chapter to them.

On one side of the large space were several pens, and running down the middle of the barn was a wide, paved aisle. They walked down it, avoiding the cow stanchions crusted with dry manure. Nick wrinkled his nose and sneezed.

"Hey, look. Here's a ladder." Brendan grabbed the first rung and began to climb up through a square hole in the ceiling. In a moment, he scrambled up into a huge hayloft with heaps of broken and disheveled bales.

Nick followed and exclaimed, "Wow! This'd make a great clubhouse. We could invite those kids from the trailer court."

"You think that's where they live?" asked Brendan.

"Sure. There weren't any cars besides ours outside the store."

"Bet they've all got bikes and could ride over here," said Brendan.

"Yeah, probably," agreed Nick. "But I think the only one we'd want to have come is Jonny. Not that silly little girl. And probably not the older one. He'd just be interested in Ami."

Brendan nodded absently. He was wandering around the hayloft, stepping gingerly because the floor felt weak in spots, almost squishy. He stared up at the massive beams. "Look at this place. I mean it's old. Probably built a couple of hundred years ago. Think of all the work that went into building it without power tools." He ran his hand along the rung of another ladder that climbed straight up and ended at a crossbeam far above their heads. The rung was worn smooth from the tread of many feet. Brendan found something reassuring about the barn.

"Hey! You guys!" Ami's voice carried up through the opening.

Nick whispered, "Let's hide."

The idea was tempting, but Brendan shook his head. He didn't feel up to games today. Especially not with their sister, who might have seen them chasing their mother's dog across the pasture.

"We're up here," he yelled.

In a moment, Ami's head appeared at the top of the ladder. She blinked and glanced around. "Where's Shag?"

"Dunno," answered Nick too quickly.

"She's around," added Brendan with a vague gesture.

Ami gave him a shrewd look as she stepped out onto

the hay. "She just better be back before Mom notices that you jerks let her loose."

"Shut up!" Nick said. "Since when do you care how Mom feels? All you think about is yourself."

Ami moved fast. She lunged forward and caught Nick off guard, slamming him down against a broken bale.

"Let me go!" he yelled. Ami had his arms pinned.

Brendan scrambled over and tried to pry her fingers loose, but they were like embedded claws. So he grabbed her ponytail and hauled back.

"Let. Go. Of. Him." Brendan gave a hard yank for each word.

"You cretin!" Ami staggered as she released Nick and twirled to face Brendan. Her features were distorted with rage, and her dark gaze swept across him, stinging like a whiplash. She raised her arm threateningly, then dropped it. Tears glistened in her eyes.

"I'm sick of you both," she said. "It's always the same. You two against me. You've always got each other."

Brendan swallowed. It was true. He couldn't imagine not having Nick. Dust particles hovered in the silence, as if listening.

"We didn't think Shag would run off," Nick said very quietly, rubbing his arm. "We tried to catch her."

"She'll come back," said Brendan, sounding more confident than he felt. "She might be immature, but she's not dumb."

"I'll find her," said Ami belligerently, then turned and climbed quickly down the ladder. They could hear her feet like angry slaps on the rungs.

Nick shrugged. "Let her go. What a brat! Jeez, this hay hurts when it's all dried out and prickly."

"We have to go with her," said Brendan. "If she finds Shag and brings her home, we'll never hear the end of it. You know Ami, Miss Rub-It-In."

Chapter Five

They followed Ami, staying at a distance, sure she'd scream at them if they got right on her heels. She trotted across the backyard and headed into the meadow.

"She knew," muttered Nick.

"She must have been watching the whole time." Brendan could picture Ami staring out the bathroom window as they let the dog escape. At least she hadn't told Mom. Not yet.

At the grove of trees, Ami turned left, crossed a short, open space, and crashed into the brush at the edge of the woods. She was swallowed by the green leaves.

Brendan looked at his brother. In the flat, bright light of the high overhead sun, his face appeared faded. Nick shrugged and asked, "You want to risk poison ivy, ticks, and maybe snakes to follow our fearless sister in hot pursuit of the missing canine?"

"Do we have a choice?"

As they plowed through the brush, Brendan tried to avoid the shiny, green leaves that he suspected were poison ivy. Within the denser growth of trees, the underbrush thinned, and they were able to see their sister. She was standing by a wide stream of rushing water, her hands on her hips, staring down, but obviously waiting for them.

"Hurry up!" Impatience made her voice shrill. "This brook will help us find Shag. We'll follow her tracks."

"What tracks? I don't see any tracks, Ami," said Brendan, shaking his head.

"Not here, idiot. We'll have to go downstream." Without explaining her logic, Ami stepped out onto a rock in the water, then jumped to another one and another.

Brendan glared at Ami's back, but he followed her. As he stepped from rock to rock, his movements were like the water—quick and flowing—only pausing at each stone before rushing on. The sound of constant gurgling filled his ears.

He felt as if he'd entered a different world of dappled shade and ceaseless motion. Each time he leaped to a new rock, he didn't know if it would teeter and tip and spill him into the water. He was constantly slightly off balance.

The brook narrowed and deepened, squeezed between rocks that became boulders. Now they were forced to scramble up and over the huge rocks along the edge, but their eyes stayed with the water. It was leading them on.

Brendan realized that the cheerful gurgling of the brook had changed to an intense muted roar that pummeled his eardrums.

"Wait!" Nick called from a short distance behind, and Brendan turned toward him.

As he bounded over to where Brendan stood, Nick said, "We should go back. We're not finding any prints, let alone Shag. I'm sick of this. And besides, Mom's going to miss us and get frantic. We don't want her calling the cops or something. Hey, Ami!"

She was five yards ahead of them, clawing up the side of a huge boulder. When she reached the top, she rose slowly to her feet and stood still, but she didn't turn toward the boys. Her back was straight and her legs slightly apart, as if she were facing a challenger.

"She won't listen," said Brendan. "We're going to have to catch her and drag her home. She's nuts." He scrambled toward her. When he reached Ami's rock, he had to search out handholds, one by one, until he dragged himself up and started to stand. Surprise made him crouch back down.

The rock was at the top of a precipice. He peered out cautiously at the white stream of water that plunged over ten feet into a pool about half the size of a tennis court. Another smaller waterfall fed into it from the left.

Nick arrived next to him, huffing and grumbling, but when he looked down, he whistled. "Looks deep enough to swim in. Let's go see."

Brendan glanced at Ami and found his attention caught by her trancelike expression. Her unblinking, blue eyes were staring into the pool. She moved away from him, closer to the edge, so that the toes of her sneakers hung over.

"Careful . . . ," Brendan whispered. He couldn't take his eyes off his sister, even though he wished he could turn away. The noise of the falls was joined by a warning inside his head. *Stop! Ami, don't move!* He screamed silently because he knew she wouldn't listen to him.

"Hey, Ami! What're you doing?" Nick asked.

Ami's hands were now stretched toward the sky, and she was prying off her sneakers with her toes.

"You can't dive!" Nick's voice was filled with panic.

Brendan reached toward her, scrambling, clutching, trying to catch her, but he wasn't fast enough.

It was a perfect dive. Ami's body arched out just far enough to avoid the curve of the boulders, and she sliced the water with hardly a splash. Brendan's mouth went dry, and his eyes stung as he watched the surface. It seemed that the ripples were all that were left of Ami—concentric circles moving rapidly outward to embrace the edge of the pool.

Suddenly Ami's head popped up. She shook strands of sopping hair from her eyes and swam in a loop with lazy, unconcerned strokes.

"You . . . you!" Nick sputtered. "You crazy psycho! Idiot! Stupid jerk!" He continued to spout ugly, angry names as he climbed down and around the rocky cliff to the side of the pool with Brendan right behind him. Ami found a shallow ledge and waded out. She wasn't smiling, but there was a contented expression on her shiny, wet face.

"It's perfect," she said very softly.

"Yeah. And you'd be perfect with a broken neck," said Brendan.

Ami pulled her ponytail forward and leaned over to wring it out. She paused and stared at the ground. "Look! A print. Right here!"

In the gravelly sand by the edge of the water was the distinct indentation of an animal's foot. Ami knelt over the track and traced it with the tip of one finger.

"What?" demanded Nick, scowling at Ami's face and then at the woods as if it, too, were somehow to blame. "You almost kill yourself, and then you want us to forget all about it and look at some dumb dog print. It probably isn't even Shag's."

Brendan stared at the animal track. It looked like most of a circle with the addition of an indented, inverted pie-shaped piece. "No dog made that," he said.

Their sister looked up. Drops of water on her eyelashes caught specks of sunlight filtering through the overhanging tree leaves. "A unicorn," she whispered.

Nick rolled his eyes. "Oh, sure, Ami. A unicorn. Right here in Pennsylvania."

"What're you talking about, Ami?" Brendan asked. "It's a horse hoofprint."

Ami got to her feet slowly, jerkily, like a marionette pulled up by its strings. Brendan wondered if she were trying to freak them out. Her eyes even looked painted, wide and staring, yet somehow, suddenly, they reminded Brendan of their father's, and he looked away. "Come on, Ami. Let's just go home."

"Yeah," agreed Nick. "Somebody was riding a horse around here and left some tracks. That's all. Big deal."

"Big deal?" Ami's voice was shrill. "You guys are so incredibly stupid! Unicorns really could exist. You ignorant fools think you know it all. But you don't. Nobody does."

Nick shook his head. "You're just trying to distract us with this unicorn garbage. But we won't forget about that insane dive you made. That pool could've been two feet deep."

"So?" said Ami defiantly.

"So? So, maybe we'll tell Mom!" Nick said.

"Go ahead. Tell!" Ami tossed her wet ponytail, and Brendan felt icy droplets hit his face. "It's too late any- how. *She* couldn't stop me. Neither could you."

Brendan shivered.

"Shut up," Nick said fiercely.

"No, I won't shut up. And as for unicorns, *I* know they're real, and I'm going to catch this one." Suddenly Ami smiled, and her voice held a threat and a note of triumph. "And you two are going to help me do it."

Nick snorted. "No way!" He began to climb up the rocks toward the top of the waterfall.

Ami started up after him. "You'll do what I say, or I'll tell Mom you let Shag loose!"

"Shag'll come back. But if you'd killed yourself, think how Mom would feel!" Nick had reached the top, and his words cascaded down, mixing with the sound of the waterfall. "You only think about yourself, Ami. It's true. I thought you'd change when Dad died."

"Stop it!" screamed Ami.

"You haven't changed. You're just the same obnox- ious sister you were before he died. And now you're acting weird . . . crazy. Unicorns are not real, Ami. Face facts!"

Ami stopped climbing. She leaned against the sheer side of the rock beside her and held her hands over her ears. "I'm not listening!" She began to hum loudly, tunelessly.

Brendan wanted to go home. Home to their apartment in New York and to the way things used to be. With Ami being a typical big sister. And Dad alive.

"I'm leaving," said Nick with a disgusted shrug. He turned and headed upstream.

It took a long time to get back to the house. Brendan passed Ami, who was moving slowly, as if the oncoming current were pushing against her, although her sneakers were as dry as his. He followed Nick from rock to rock. When he glanced back a few times, he could see Ami's pale, blank face. She had undone her hair, and the tangled, wet strands swung out to the side as she leaped to each new rock. She didn't ask them to wait or slow down, even though they got far ahead.

Chapter Six

They went in the back door but avoided looking at Shag's empty chain. In the hallway, they had to navigate around boxes and a haphazard stack of chairs. Their mother greeted them in the kitchen where she was unpacking utensils. "I was beginning to get worried," she said. She still wore her scarf, but tendrils of hair had escaped. "What time is it anyhow?"

"Past lunchtime," said Nick quickly.

"Where's Ami?" Mom looked anxiously around them toward the doorway.

"She's going upstairs to change," Nick said. "She got a little wet in the creek."

"Oh, well." Mom nodded. She looked dazed as she rummaged through a carton on the counter. "What a mess. The movers didn't organize anything. They kept asking me, 'Where do you want this item, ma'am,' and I just didn't know what to tell them."

"So," said Nick, "what's for lunch? I see the new fridge arrived." He yanked open the door and stuck his head inside. "Ah, it's working, but . . ." From across the room, Brendan could see it was empty except for the quart of milk they had bought the day before and been keeping in the cooler.

"Peanut butter," Brendan said. "There's always that."

"No." Their mother shook her head emphatically. "There's some canned stew in this box right here." She thumped the side of a cardboard carton with her fist. "As soon as I find the can opener, we'll have a real meal. It'll be supper and lunch combined—'lupper,' or whatever. In the meantime, have some crackers."

Brendan stuffed three saltines into his mouth and followed Nick into the living room. It looked as confusing as the kitchen. "Hey, the TV!" Nick glanced around at the piles of boxes. "Where's the remote?" Finally, he walked over and hit the switch. The TV came on, but they soon learned that only three channels were clear enough to watch. Nick rummaged around and found the VCR. When they tried to hook it up, they couldn't get it to work.

"We're sunk," muttered Nick. "We can't watch tapes, and we only get a couple of lame channels. And Mom had to go and give away Dad's computer just 'cause her friend who volunteers at that animal shelter said *they* needed one. Like *we* don't? What'll we do all summer?"

"Come on," Brendan said with a shrug. "Let's check out upstairs."

They discovered that each of their rooms was crammed with furniture and other belongings. Brendan used his foot to poke at a large stack of boxes, some labeled "Twins" in their mother's scrawl. After ripping open a few of them, he dumped their contents in a jumble on his floor—used school notebooks, tattered picture books and paperbacks, toys that looked old and sorry, pens and pencils with no erasers. He sorted the items into several piles, rocked back on his heels, and sighed. Where could he put all this stuff? There was only one high shelf in the closet, and he had no bookcase. In their New York apartment, there had been a whole wall in their room devoted to shelves.

Now he looked at the partition separating his room from Nick's. He noticed again the uneven plaster and the missing chips here and there. All the walls definitely needed to be painted. But after that, who would put up the shelves? That had been Dad's job—tapping along the wall, listening for a change in pitch to determine where to place the screws. Mom could do it, maybe. Or he and Nick.

Brendan examined his hands and tried to picture them using a hammer to tap, holding a screwdriver, placing a shelf. But instead of his own hands, he saw his father's strong fingers and blunt nails.

Blinking quickly, he stood up and grabbed the post of the bed. Wait a minute. Was this the right bed? Yes, here were his initials where he'd carved them on the edge of the headboard when he was eight. Each year he'd added his age. His parents had never noticed. Or, at least, they'd never said anything. January a year ago, on his and Nick's eleventh birthday, he'd carved a simple "11." But this year, he hadn't even thought about adding a twelve.

He stared at the eleven. A good number, he thought

now, leaning his head down to peer at the two straight lines. Easy to carve. Two digits exactly alike. Identical. Like me and Nick. We won't be an age like that again until we're 22 and then 33. Brendan imagined the numbers skipping through time, over a decade at each jump. What would he be like at 44? Suddenly he shivered.

Forty-four. That was the age Dad had been when he died. He'd been riding his bike to work and had an accident. An accident. It sounded so simple. Almost harmless. People had accidents all the time and survived them. Why did *he* have to die?

"Hey, Brendan!" Nick stood in the doorway. "Whoa. You sure haven't got much done. I got the wrong dresser. You want to switch the whole thing or just our stuff?" He waved one of Brendan's old T-shirts in his hand.

They decided to trade the drawers and went back and forth, bumping into each other in the narrow hallway.

After shoving Nick's last drawer into place, Brendan looked around his brother's room. It was nearly the same size as his own. The location of the door and the two small windows was similar, although his own had the extra window at the back of the house. But this room was different for another reason. It had its own identity. Nick had already found some tape and covered one wall with posters of basketball stars and fancy cars. His bed was sloppily made with an old green blanket, and he'd even managed to locate a clean pillowcase.

"I've got our old Legos," Nick said, waving toward a neatly organized corner of boxes. "All of them. I'll keep 'em in my room if you'll keep all the puzzles. You want me to help you now? I'm just about done here."

Brendan shrugged but didn't protest when his brother followed him back to his room. Nick looked around critically. "Can't you find some posters?"

"I think you got 'em all."

"Oh yeah, maybe." Nick raised the lid on the school desk. They each had one, bought at an auction several years ago. "Hey, this one is mine!" He pointed to the underside of the lid. "See? Here's where I painted Susan Brinkley's name when she moved away in fifth grade. Here're my baseball cards. They're all messed up. . . ."

"O.K., we'll switch," offered Brendan. They charged each other in the hallway, slamming the metal desk fronts together with a satisfying clang. Then they backed up and did it again.

"Boys!" Mom's voice was threatening, so they moved the desks quickly into the proper rooms without any more bumper car activity.

"I'll help you later on," Nick said from his room. "I gotta straighten out these cards. You got anything else of mine?"

"Don't know yet." Brendan stared at the heap of sports equipment on the floor of his closet. It looked out of place—useless in this new environment. He could not see himself dribbling a basketball or even tossing a football in the overgrown yard.

Brendan turned from the closet and glared at the boxes yet to be unpacked. Maybe he could just hide some of this stuff. Grabbing an unlabeled carton, he attempted to lift it onto the shelf at the top of his closet. Too heavy!

What's in this anyhow? he wondered. When he set it down and pried it open, he discovered another box inside, labeled in Ami's bold printing with the warning "Keep Out!" But this box had split open, and Mom must have put it into the carton to keep it from falling apart.

Within the box, Brendan saw books, and he couldn't resist prying the split corner open just a little more to find out what they were about. They all sounded like fantasies—several with "Unicorn" in their titles. He struggled to free one book and then opened it. On the first blank page, in their father's tall, thin handwriting, Brendan read, "For Ami. Happy tenth birthday. May all your dreams, of unicorns or whatever, come true. Love, Mom and Dad." Brendan tried to shove it back between the other books, but a spiral notebook got in the way. With a grunt, he pulled the notebook out and sat staring at it. Obviously, it belonged to Ami. He should just put it back and take the whole stupid box to her. Now.

So what favors has Ami done for me lately? he thought. Without another moment of hesitation, he opened the notebook. The pages were filled with Ami's neat hand-writing—every bit of it about unicorns. His eyes caught on various headings: Characteristics, Habitat, History, Powers, and Capture.

He found himself reading portions, learning about unicorns. Here it said that they had cloven hooves. So, was that animal track we saw by the pool cloven or what? Who knows? he thought. The most interesting information was under the "Powers" heading. It told about the healing strength of the unicorn's horn and its potential to grant immortality.

Immortality? Not dying, right? Brendan felt an eerie tingling at the back of his neck. But he couldn't make himself stop skimming the words. Here was stuff about capturing a unicorn and how it was easy with the help of a pure young maiden. All you had to do was get this maiden to go out and sit under a tree, and some dumb unicorn would come along and put its head in her lap. That wasn't quite how Ami wrote it, but that was the general idea.

Pure young woman? Ami? Silly. A fantasy for little kids, he told himself. Abruptly, almost angrily, he pushed the notebook back between the other books and clapped shut the flaps on the outside carton. Then he shoved it out of his door and across the hallway. "Hey, Ami," he said loudly. "This is yours." Her door was shut, and he was glad he didn't have to talk to her.

He went back into his own room and stared at the mess.

"Ami! Nick and Brendan! Have you kids seen Shag?"

Brendan's stomach gave a guilty lurch as his mother poked her head in his door.

"I was so sure I'd tied her up just fine," Mom said. "But she's gone. Looks as if she got that hook undone. Somehow. I should have noticed that she wasn't even barking at the movers."

"I don't know where she is," Brendan said truthfully. He sat down on his bed and listened to his mother's voice as she went to Ami's room and then Nick's. She sounded apologetic as she told them each how the dog had gotten loose. Then he heard her go downstairs and outside to call for Shag. Over and over until Brendan wanted to cover his ears.

Finally, Mom came inside and yelled hoarsely up to them, "All of you come on downstairs. I've made that stew and some pudding for dessert. Sorry it's so late."

They ate in the kitchen at their old table, sandwiched between cartons and heaps of unpacked objects. Brendan found himself staring at a green vase decorated with purple flowers and labeled "AMI" in wobbly letters. Probably she'd made it in kindergarten. Where had that thing been in their apartment? he wondered as he chewed the chunks of meat, trying to ignore the taste of the can.

Nick was carefully picking through his stew, moving all the peas to one side of his plate so he wouldn't accidentally eat one. Ami wasn't eating at all. She had stayed in her room despite their mother's repeated invitations.

There were two flavors of pudding, vanilla and butterscotch, swirled together in a big bowl.

"Butterscotch is Ami's favorite," said Mom.

"I think," said Nick, holding his spoon upside down and watching to see how long before the dollop of pudding slipped off onto his plate, "she's on the road to becoming anorexic."

"Don't say that." Mom's voice sounded tight.

"Well, really, she's sort of . . . weird sometimes, even for a teenager," said Nick. "You know, Mom, you gotta admit it."

Brendan watched their mother. She had been sitting stiffly in the straight-backed chair with her hands resting on either side of her plate. Now she slid her palms to the edge of the table and gripped it with her thumbs. He could see the tension in her tightened fingers.

"You talk too much," he said to Nick, trying to keep his tone light.

Nick nodded. "Yeah, maybe so, but . . ."

Mom abruptly leaped up from the table and rushed into the hallway.

"See? She's upset," whispered Brendan fiercely. "Lay off."

But she was back in a moment, her face flushed. "I thought I heard Shag." She slid wearily into her chair. "I just don't see how I could have been so stupid. I thought that hook was fine. Guess I should have bought a new collar or something. It must have been too old and worn to hold up to her jumping around."

Brendan stared down at his pudding. He knew he was avoiding looking at Nick, but he couldn't tear his eyes off the puddle of pudding next to the greasy smear left from the stew.

Nick cleared his throat. "Uh . . . Mom? I did it. I let Shag loose. I thought she'd stay with us. But she took off. We all looked and looked for her but couldn't find her. I'm sorry."

Brendan swallowed. He had to hand it to Nick. Admitting such a mistake wasn't easy.

"Oh." That's all Mom said.

Brendan squirmed in his seat as he gulped down the last of his pudding. When he and Nick got up to put their plates in the sink, Mom stayed rigid in her chair. Her voice held a touch of bitterness as she said, "Seems as if I just can't hang onto anything. . . ."

"Mom, I said I was sorry," Nick mumbled.

"I know. It's just . . . never mind." Mom shoved her plate away, and it clunked into Ami's old vase.

Later Brendan said to Nick, "It's O.K. Mom'll forgive you, and now Ami won't be able to hold that over our heads. Besides, Shag'll come back in a day or two."

But she didn't.

Chapter Seven

The next three days, they spent hours driving around, stopping at all the nearby houses to ask if anyone had seen a medium-sized, blond-and-white, shaggy dog with a happy grin.

Brendan stayed in the car, feeling slightly embarrassed by his mother but not wanting to tell her. Nick still looked guilty, but that didn't get him out of the car either.

At least we go along, thought Brendan, while Ami hides at home.

Each time Mom returned to the car after talking to some neighbor, she looked more discouraged. "I dropped the line about her grinning," she told them finally. "It was making me too sad. Besides, no one knew what I meant. She did—does—grin, though, right?"

"Mom . . ." Nick stopped, at a loss for words for once.

She sighed. "At least I'm meeting people around here. I wish I had a map. Some roads or driveways look like cow paths, and I'm afraid to drive up them."

Brendan thought that by now they'd been everywhere, but no one in the neighborhood had seen Shag. She might be dead. Hit by a car and maybe knocked off into the weeds so they wouldn't see her. He shuddered, thinking of the dead raccoons and squirrels they saw each day on the roads. The animals' bodies were in various stages of decay or, if freshly killed, bloated and bloodstained. He found himself averting his eyes whenever a lump of fur appeared in the distance. But usually, at the last second, he'd glance back to assure himself that the body was not Shag's. On the third day, just as they approached their own lane, they saw a dead cat. Its cream-colored fur nearly made Brendan's heart stop before his brain registered that the animal was way too small to be their dog.

"That's it." Mom cleared her throat. "No more driving all over. We'll move on to plan B."

The next morning, she made beautiful posters with clear, large lettering and a drawing of Shag, grinning. The boys helped her tack them to bulletin boards at several spots in the neighboring town. On the way home, they stopped and taped one to the window of the store near the trailer court.

Mom called the local newspaper to place an ad. "It won't be in the Lost and Found section until next week," she told the boys. "The paper only comes out on Thursdays. I guess it's too late, even though it's just Tuesday." She sighed. "What sort of place is this with a *weekly* paper?"

"A place with no news," said Nick.

By Friday morning, their mother acted determined not to mention the dog. "I need a *New York Times,*" she announced after breakfast. "I mean, how can I drink coffee without it? We'll go to town together and get a paper. And we'll do a little exploring. Ami, you, too."

"No way." Ami was sprawled on the couch in front of the TV, hitting the remote button over and over. The screen barely had time to register an image before it was zapped away and a new one appeared. "Crap! There's nothing on this stupid thing!"

"Ami!" Mom shouted. "I . . . I'm so sick of seeing you just sitting and doing nothing. You haven't been helping at all. Today you'll do as I say. You are coming along to town."

"Mom. No." Ami leaned back and yawned. The TV was now tuned to a channel that was nothing but a mass of moving dots and static.

"Why not?" Mom asked, an angry edge to her voice. "You can't just sit here, day after day."

"I *can.* And I *will.* Just stay out of my face, Mom."

"Ami! What has gotten into you?" When there was no reply, Mom went on, suddenly sounding defeated, "I'm just trying . . . I don't want you to sit at home alone. That's all. Really."

"Makes more sense than racing around this hick place and sticking up lost-dog posters. She isn't coming back. She's dead!" Brendan thought he heard a catch in Ami's voice. She loved Shag, too. But her tone was sharp as she added, "Give it up, Mom."

"I can't," Mom said softly. "And I wasn't even talking about the dog, Ami. You know that."

"Oh, this is about *me,* is it? Well, then, don't worry. *I'm* fine." She jabbed a button on the remote. The TV burst into life on a functioning channel, its volume turned on high, drowning out words but not thoughts.

On the way to town, Brendan and Nick were quiet. When their mother parked the car, they both hopped out and followed her into the pharmacy. They trailed her up and down the aisles. She picked up a bottle of suntan lotion, stared at it, then muttered, "Insect repellent, where is it?"

"Over there, Mom." Nick pointed to a prominent display.

As she examined the various brands and read the labels, the pharmacist behind the high counter watched her with a faint smile.

Don't you have anything better to do? Brendan thought, glaring at him.

As if she felt the man's gaze, Mom suddenly looked up and said, "Oh, could I have a *New York Times,* please?"

"I'm sorry, ma'am, we only get the Sunday edition. And not too many of those. We just order enough for our regulars because there's not much demand." He shook his head in apology. "I'll ask for an extra one next week, if you'd like."

"Oh, thanks. I'll come back on Sunday. I'll just take a local paper now."

"Over there, ma'am, on that rack. It comes out on Thursdays only."

"Yes, I know." Mom frowned.

"Can I help you with anything else?" the pharmacist

asked pleasantly. He smiled broadly, revealing a gap between his large front teeth.

"How 'bout some stuff for poison ivy, Mom?" said Nick helpfully. "I've got this rash on my wrist, and it's itching awful."

"Some cortisone cream would do nicely." The man came out from behind the counter and pointed to several small boxes on a nearby shelf. "Nasty stuff, poison ivy."

Brendan stared at the neatly stitched label on the pocket of the man's white coat. Jim Latchall, pharmacist. Why did he have to stand so close to Mom? Brendan suddenly felt like shoving him against the shelves. He pictured the bottles of vitamins and boxes of creams flipping up and landing on Jim Latchall's head—right where the longish hairs were neatly combed to cover the bald spot.

Mom just nodded vaguely and kept looking at the various anti-itch medications. She reached out and chose a bottle of pink calamine lotion.

"Ah, the old standby," said the pharmacist approvingly, as if their mother were a genius.

Mom counted out money to pay, then said, "Since I didn't get my *Times,* maybe we should go to the library." She glanced at the pharmacist. "Could you give us directions?"

Jim Latchall stood there, his hand perilously close to their mother's shoulder as he gestured and explained the library's location. "You go out here on First Street and down to Dotters Road and then turn . . ."

Brendan tuned out the man's words and watched

him closely. When he motioned with his left hand, there was no wedding ring. But that didn't necessarily mean anything, right? This is ridiculous, he told himself. Mom isn't going to run off with this guy.

"You won't have any trouble finding it, I don't think," finished the pharmacist.

After Mom had assured him that they'd do fine, he asked, "You people new around here?"

What business is it of yours? Brendan thought. He could see from Nick's expression that he was asking the same silent question.

But Mom just nodded. "Uh, yes. We've moved into Martin Ferguson's farmhouse."

"Oh! You know, I think I heard about a niece who inherited the place, right?"

Mom nodded quickly and said, "That's me. Thanks so much for your help."

When they were back in the stuffy car, Nick remarked, "This small-town business is kind of spooky." He held up the local newspaper and pretended to read the headlines. "New York Woman and Kids Move into Old Shack."

"It's not that bad, is it?" Mom asked anxiously. "I think the house is fine."

"Mom, I was joking. It's just this nosy stuff is so different from New York."

"You're right, Nick," she said with a sigh. "We've been here how long? A little over a week? And already we're tangled in the grapevine. But it can't be helped. And maybe having a gossip network will get Shag back. Now, which street did he say to turn on?"

Of course they hadn't been listening. So, after seeing more of the small town than they really wanted, they arrived at the single-story brick building. Inside, Brendan was pleased to discover books by some of his favorite authors. They signed up for library cards and left with their arms loaded.

Their last stop was at the local hardware store, where Mom bought wall paint, rollers, and brushes. On the way home, Brendan paged through several of the library books, trying to decide which to read first. Nick busied himself with the local newspaper, spreading it wide so the pages flapped in the wind from the open windows. "Mom, we've got to get the A/C fixed in this car," he said.

Mom didn't answer, and Brendan wondered if she'd started thinking about Shag again.

When they passed the trailer court, Nick remarked, "Let's ride our bikes over there when we get home. See if we can find those kids we met the other day."

"First we'll have some lunch," Mom said. "And you guys be careful on this road. It's got hardly any room for bikes. Be sure to wear your helmets."

For a moment, there was silence in the car as everyone avoided thinking or saying anything more about the dangers of bike riding. Then Mom went on quickly, "Tomorrow I want you to start on the lawn. I asked the auctioneer to save a mower. He told me there were two of them, so one's got to be around somewhere. If we don't get that grass hacked away, it's going to take over the house."

And there will be Ami, Brendan thought, asleep on

the couch while the weeds grow tall and tangled, covering the walls, the roof. When she wakes up in a hundred years, will she be different?

As they drove up their long driveway, Brendan listened to the now-familiar swish of grass beneath the car. He breathed carefully and tried not to look too soon toward the house. Toward the porch where he hoped to see Shag. But there was no furry shape huddled there or hurtling toward them with excited barks. No Perpetual Pup.

Only old Shere Khan greeted them with a raspy mew when they went in the front door. He didn't even move from his indentation on the couch.

Ami sat up. She looked as if she'd been asleep, but she watched them dump their library books on the coffee table. Mom asked hopefully, "Any phone calls about Shag?"

Ignoring her, Ami said, "You went to the library? Why didn't you tell me! I've been wanting to go. Nobody ever tells me anything!" She catapulted off the couch and flung herself out of the room. Brendan could hear her sharp stomps down the hallway, then on the stairs, and finally the slam of her door.

Mom sighed and retreated to the kitchen.

"How about if we write up a schedule of activities each day," said Nick sarcastically. "That way Ami won't be left out." Brendan rolled his eyes.

Mom made lunch, but Ami didn't even answer when called, so the rest of the family ate without her. Brendan and Nick decided to put off their trip to the trailer court. It seemed wrong to leave Mom when Ami was in such a bad mood. They lay around the living room all afternoon, engrossed in their library books. Supper was dismal, with no one wanting to say anything about Ami's absence from yet another meal. The boys did the dishes, grumbling to each other about their shirking sister, and then returned to the living room.

When the light began to fade, Mom wandered in and said sadly, "What do you suppose Ami meant by nobody telling her anything? I tried to get her to go along, didn't I?"

"Yeah, you did. She probably just wanted books on unicorns," said Nick.

"What?" Mom asked in a distracted voice.

"Nothing," said Brendan.

"Look," Mom said abruptly. She pointed at the window. The three of them moved closer to stare out at the front lawn. The air above the tall grass was twinkling with fireflies. "Lovely, aren't they?" she whispered. "Remember how you kids liked to catch them and put them in jars? And your dad always made you set them free. One time Ami said good-bye to each one by name as it flew away. Funny thing, I didn't even *think* about fireflies this year. And . . . yet . . . here they are."

Later that night, Shere Khan woke Brendan with his incessant purring. Still half asleep, Brendan staggered up and went to the bathroom. When he returned to his room, he peered out his back window to check on the fireflies. He saw only a few blinking hesitantly at this late hour. All his windows were open, but Mom had insisted he stick old-fashioned wood-rimmed screens in them. Pressing his nose against the wire mesh, he smelled dust and metal. Then he heard a sound, almost like a sighing in the grass. He listened intently as he stared at the backyard.

A figure moved into view, illuminated in the pale light from Mom's downstairs studio window. It was Ami. She was singing in a high, quavering voice, and she was wearing something long that hung down her back. As he watched, she reached toward a blinking firefly. For a moment, the light from the window bathed her face. Brendan drew back, thinking she would see him watching. But she went on singing and twirling, and then he noticed that she was holding a glass jar. Inside it fireflies blinked off and on, their light a faint, greenish glow. Probably dying. Brendan went back to bed, but it took him a long time to go to sleep.

Chapter Eight

In a weathered shed nearly hidden in weeds behind the barn, Brendan and Nick found an old-fashioned push lawn mower. The blades turned and clattered purposefully as they wheeled it into the morning sunlight. Later, when Brendan actually set to work, shoving the machine repeatedly against the tall grass in the front yard, he knew why no one had bought it.

"Might as well chew this stuff off with my teeth," he told himself and wished he were inside painting the living room with Nick and his mother. He could feel blisters rising on his palms, and with each push forward, his shoulders jarred in their sockets. He'd only been working for half an hour, and already his body felt bruised. He stopped and pried a clump of mangled grass from the blades.

"How come you're quitting?" asked Nick, coming out the front door. He looked cool and unruffled. "Is *that* all you got done? I've painted more square feet of wall than you've mowed. Not fair!"

"Right. Trade ya," offered Brendan quickly. He turned his back on the tiny mowed space and walked up the stone path to the house.

"Hey, wait a sec," yelled Nick, but Brendan ignored him.

Inside the living room, the smell of latex paint mingled with the odor of freshly chopped grass. He looked at the deep turquoise wall his mother was finishing. "That's kind of dark, isn't it, Mom?"

"Not to worry. The other three walls are going to be white. This is an accent color."

Mom had taken down the drapes and put them on the wooden floor and across furniture. They were speckled with paint. "Drop cloths," she said, waving one arm. "We don't need drapes anyhow. I mean, who's going to be looking in at us way out here in the middle of nowhere?" She smiled at Brendan, then frowned. "You look hot. Go in the kitchen and get something cool to drink."

Ami was there, slouched at the table, her hair unbrushed. She was wearing the same clothes as the day before.

"So what've you been doing?" Brendan didn't try to keep the annoyance out of his voice. He wanted to ask her about last night and the fireflies, but her sullen manner discouraged him.

Ami just grunted and took another sip of lemonade.

"It's really not right, Ami. You could help, too."

"Why? She's got you two paragons of helpfulness. Besides, what is it with Mom anyhow? All this cleaning and junk? What's she doing, nesting or something?"

Brendan found a glass on the counter, rinsed it out, and poured himself some lemonade. He pulled out a chair and sat down. Maybe Mom was just keeping busy so she wouldn't have time to think and remember. He didn't share this idea with Ami.

71

"Nesting," Ami said as if that were decided. Then she added in an ugly tone, "Well, this little fledgling is sick of the nest." She gave her glass a shove. It tipped over and rolled across the table. Brendan caught it just before it fell off.

"Thanks so much," Ami said sarcastically.

"You want to break a glass, why don't you just throw it against the wall, Ami?" He spoke through clenched teeth. "That would really get Mom's attention. Is that what you want? You want Mom to freak out?"

Ami swore at him, then said, "You *twins* are the ones that let the dog loose. In case you've forgotten. It's your fault. She's probably lying dead in a ditch somewhere."

Brendan swallowed the words that leaped into his mind. Not me. I didn't do it. He gulped his drink. He could barely hear the sporadic clatter of the lawn mower and Nick's unintelligible curses. He stared at the tabletop. There was the spot in the grain of the wood that looked like a small deer. He'd noticed that when he was about five and had always tried to sit so the deer was facing him and not upside down. Now he ran his fingers along the edge of the table and felt a rough, scratchy patch. He'd grown up with these small, familiar things. Now they were here, in this different place. Like their dad's chair sitting in a corner of the living room heaped with one of the dusty drapes.

The rug from their apartment living room was rolled up, waiting for the painting to be done. Later, when it was spread out, there would be the frayed corner that Shag had chewed as a puppy. But where was

Shag? And where was Dad? He felt the sweat on his brow turn cool, and he shivered.

Ami got up from the table and started out the door to the hallway. She stopped and looked back at him. "I'm going to the pool. Now. You can tell Mom if you want." Her tone was without expression, yet it held a threat. She turned and headed out the back door.

What was she planning this time? Or was she just trying to get out of working? It wasn't fair that he and Nick kept getting stuck with all the chores. When Brendan returned to the living room, Mom asked, "How're you guys doing on the lawn?"

Before he could reply, Nick slammed in the front door. "Mom! We have to buy a power mower!"

"I guess that's my answer."

"I bet we can get a good one at the hardware store," said Nick. "You want to go now?"

"No, I have to finish this wall."

Brendan wiped his palms on his cutoffs and said, "Listen, Mom? Ami just told me she's going to go wading in that brook in the woods. Can Nick and I go, too? We've been helping lots more than she has."

"I guess you're right. You two have been very helpful." Mom took one more swipe at the wall with the paint roller. "O.K., you can go. Have fun."

The walk through the creek to the pool, with Ami somewhere ahead of them, seemed shorter than it had been before. When they were nearly there, they heard a different sound mixed with the rushing gurgle of the falls.

"Who do you think that is?" asked Nick.

Brendan shrugged. There were voices, but it was

hard to tell anything else. Maybe Ami's really gone nuts and is having a conversation with the waterfall, Brendan thought.

They approached cautiously, climbing to the top of the falls slowly, listening. Brendan looked down at the water. Three children were swimming. He recognized Ami's blond head, and then, as the others looked up and waved, he realized that they were two of the kids from the store, Jonny and Sandy.

For just a fraction of a second, he wondered why they were here, in what he'd assumed was *their* place. But, of course, it made sense. The trailer court wasn't any farther from here than their house, probably closer.

"Come on in!" yelled Jonny. "Jump! It's plenty deep."

Brendan stared down at the sun-speckled surface and swallowed quickly as if to fill the emptiness in his stomach. He pulled off his sneakers, then stretching his arms out, he took a gulp of air, held it, and jumped.

Straight down. The air rushing past. An icy crash into the water. He opened his eyes and swam through the greenish haze to burst the shadowed surface. Nick had followed him into the water and came up beside him. "Cold!" Nick began to splash Jonny and threaten to dunk Sandy.

"Hey, you guys like Swallow Hole?" asked Jonny.

"Is that what it's called?" asked Brendan, treading water.

"I think it's named for barn swallows," said Jonny. "You know, those birds that like to build their nests in barns? But my brother says it's Swallow Whole, with a W. Like this water can swallow you whole."

"Nice idea," said Nick, grinning at Sandy. The little girl stuck out her tongue and swam toward Ami, who was climbing out of the water.

"Hey! What's your name?" demanded Sandy.

"I'm Ami," she said and surprised Brendan by smiling. She stretched out in a spot of sun.

"Come on. Race you to the falls," Jonny said.

Brendan got there first because Nick and Jonny were trying to shove each other underwater. He pulled himself up onto slippery rocks to sit beneath the sparkling spill of the waterfall.

"Agghh!" yelled Nick as he and Jonny arrived. "Talk about a cold shower!"

Jonny tipped his head back and let the water fill his mouth. He spat it at Nick.

Brendan drew back farther into the cool recess behind the falls and huddled there, trying to stare through the screen of water. The scene was distorted, but he could make out the smear of orange that was Ami's T-shirt. She was still sunning herself on a large rock.

"So," said Jonny, "how'd you guys find this place? It's private property, you know."

"Oh yeah?" said Nick. "Whose? Yours?"

"We got no property," said Jonny. "Just our trailer. This is Old Man Johansson's land. He lives way, way up the hill. Only comes down about once a month to get groceries. Wears old floppy boots. Galoshes, my mom calls them. And a dirty flannel shirt even when it's a hundred in the shade. The guy is one brick short of a load. I guess his wife had cancer and died real slow and bad. Our mom's a nurse and works in the ER, and she

75

saw her a couple of times. Said she looked like a skeleton. You know. Toward the end. When she finally died, the old man freaked out."

Sandy popped her head under the waterfall. "You talking about Old Man Johansson? He tried to kill my friend Clair's big sister. She was just minding her own business. Catching bugs for school."

"For biology class," Jonny explained.

"Shut up. Let me tell it. Anyhow, she was, like, real close to his house and all of a sudden, *Boom!* He shoots his gun at her and starts screaming about tres . . . whatever that word is."

"Trespassing."

Sandy glared at Jonny. Then, as if she'd exhausted that topic, she turned back to Nick and asked with concern, "You find your dog yet?"

Nick shook his head. "How'd you know about that?"

"We saw those posters," said Jonny. "And one of our neighbors said you'd come by asking about the dog when we weren't home."

"We have a dog," said Sandy. "She's a laboodle. Named Panda."

Jonny said, "She's part Lab and part poodle. We got her when our neighbor's poodle had pups. But she's got the dumbest name for an all-black dog."

"Just 'cause I named her," Sandy said, "that's why you think it's dumb."

"You read my mind," said Jonny. His sister cupped her hands so the falling water shot into his face, and then she dove out of sight.

"Sisters," he muttered. "Who needs 'em?"

"Yeah," Nick said. "Ours was making us look for paw prints and stuff. So we can track our dog, but we've only found a horse hoofprint."

"You know anybody who's got a horse around here?" asked Brendan.

"No. Nobody," said Jonny. "You sure it wasn't a cow print? Sometimes Miller's cows get loose. One time I woke up and looked out my window into all these cow snouts, snuffling at the screen. Like they wanted to eat it or something. I thought sure they'd tip the whole trailer over."

"It was a horse. I think," said Nick. "Right over there next to the water."

"Here? By Swallow Hole?" said Jonny. "No way. Why would anybody ride a horse in these woods? Too many rocks and branches. You'd get your head knocked off."

"Maybe it was alone. A stray," suggested Brendan.

"Sounds crazy to me," said Jonny, shaking his head. Then he did a shallow dive through the falls into the pool.

Not as crazy as a unicorn, Brendan thought. His teeth were beginning to chatter, and his arms and legs were a mass of goose bumps. He slipped back into the water, but that didn't help. He wished for a sun-drenched, sandy beach or at least the hot concrete next to a real swimming pool. He tried paddling in circles, but the chill was seeping into his bones, and he climbed out and crawled up onto a relatively flat rock some distance from where Ami lay. Jonny and Nick were still laughing and talking in the water.

Sandy continued to yell and splash at them. Finally, Jonny went after her, pushed her head under for a few seconds, and then let her up, sputtering. He said right in her face, "Leave us alone!" She stuck out her tongue, then paddled away and climbed up next to Ami.

Jonny still sounded annoyed as he turned to Nick and said, loudly enough for his little sister to hear him, "One time I overheard our mom tell a friend of hers that Sandy was an accident. Wonder how it feels to be an *accident?*" But Sandy turned her back and hunched her shoulders. Suddenly Brendan felt sorry for her. He knew just how she felt. He remembered something that had happened a few years before—something he had hoped to forget.

It had been New Year's Eve, and their parents were having a party at their apartment. He and Nick had stayed in their room for a while, away from the boring adult conversation. But hunger drove them out. Nick reached the living room first and headed straight for the table laden with goodies. Just as Brendan came through the doorway and was winding his way around and between the guests, he saw Dad motion toward Nick and heard him say, "Nicholas, come over here and meet Larry Rosenberg." Dad was smiling, a drink in one hand, and when he saw Brendan, he said, "Oh, and here comes the clone." It seemed to Brendan that the room became very quiet. Dad shook his head. "Only kidding. These are our twins. Identical. Bet you can't tell them apart, Larry." But Brendan hadn't stayed around for Larry to test his skills.

Back in their room, Nick had laughed and said, "Hey, I never thought of it that way. You're my clone 'cause I was born first." The look Brendan gave him made him add quickly, "Forget it. Dad was just teasing." No one mentioned the incident again. But Brendan had not been able to forget.

"Hey, listen!" Jonny said loudly. "I think that's Greg coming."

Brendan huddled within the circle of his shivering arms. He felt overexposed in a pair of drenched cutoffs and lots of wet skin. He wished he'd brought a towel. But that would have made Mom suspect that they'd planned on more than wading.

Jonny's older brother came out of the woods. He wasn't wearing a shirt, and all his muscles were in plain sight. He walked into shallow water between some rocks and began swinging his arms back and forth, letting the tips of his fingers brush the surface.

"Greggie!" yelled Sandy as she danced up and down. "Come on and give me a piggy ride."

Ami looked at Greg and smiled vaguely. He dipped his head toward her, ignoring Sandy. Then he made a shallow dive that took him to the middle of the pool. In a moment, Ami followed him.

Still talking, Nick and Jonny climbed up on a rock next to Brendan. He wished they'd shut up. Ami was saying something to Greg, but he couldn't quite make out the words. Then she was coming out of the water, Greg right behind her. Brendan blinked. She looked too thin but still awfully grown up, her wet T-shirt clinging to her chest and her shorts dripping water down her long, slender legs. She leaned down and pointed to the ground.

"Maybe a horse or a cow," Greg said. "That's what it looks like to me."

Ami pulled a wet strand of hair back from her face. "I'm sure it's a unicorn."

"A unicorn?" Greg swung his arms aimlessly, and then he smiled, as if he thought Ami were sharing a secret joke with him. "You're into fantasy? I like some science fiction, but fantasy's just too far out. What I like most is nonfiction books and movies that are more or less realistic."

"Boring," said Ami. "You like boring stuff, so maybe you're boring, too."

Greg smiled at her. "No way. I'm not boring."

"So, what's that supposed to mean?" asked Ami.

"Ah, come on. You know," Greg said in a teasing tone of voice.

Ami tossed her hair and giggled.

Brendan wrapped his arms more tightly around his cold legs and watched Ami in action. She was acting normal for a change—flirting like a regular teenager—but he had an unsettled feeling in the pit of his stomach.

"Let's swim some more," said Greg.

Ami shrugged her shoulders and shook her head. "It's too cold."

"Is not!" Greg stepped back into the water and splashed some toward Ami.

Laughing, she jumped in beside him and tossed a handful of water into his face.

"Hey! We're both wet, so let's go to the waterfall,"

Greg said, reaching out and grabbing Ami's hand. She pulled back a little as if in play. But when Greg didn't let go and tried to drag her deeper into the pool, Ami abruptly wrenched free.

She shook her head fiercely, her eyes like bright shards of blue glass. "Don't touch me." Her voice had gone cold. "I am a maiden of pure heart, and I *will* capture the unicorn."

Her words were met with silence. It seemed to Brendan that even the birds were quiet for a moment. Then Greg shrugged. "Whatever you say." He looked toward Sandy, then at Jonny. "Mom wants you two home. You know she doesn't like you guys swimming here. She told me to get you. Let's go."

"Do we have to?" asked Sandy.

"Yeah. Now," Greg said gruffly as if to cover his embarrassment.

Jonny grinned and waved at Ami. "See you around, Miss Pure Heart," he said as he scrambled over the rocks.

"Ah, leave her alone," muttered Greg with a glance toward Ami. A hesitant smile flickered on his lips.

But Ami didn't seem to notice. "There *is* a unicorn," she said a moment after Greg had turned away to follow his brother and sister along the path. She might have been talking to herself, although Brendan was sure Greg, Jonny, and Sandy heard her loud and clear. He wished he could clap his hands over everyone's ears—including his own.

Chapter Nine

The following five days, it rained. The sky hung low and gray and dripped steadily. There was no thunder, just a bleak wetness that reminded Brendan of sadness—like the dull ache that had engulfed him after their father died, when nothing could break through, neither happiness nor sun.

When he and Nick raced down the lane each morning to collect the mail from the rusty mailbox, his slicker felt icy against the bare skin of his arms. It was too wet for exploring, and Ami made no mention of tracking Shag or unicorns. So they spent the days inside, the sky pressing down like a soggy blanket, holding them in place. They didn't want to ride bikes in the rain, and so they didn't go to the trailer court. Nick complained bitterly about the lack of a VCR. Mom wasn't listening.

On the second day of the rain, she had abruptly quit organizing, despite the stray items and cartons that remained stacked in corners. She had located her yarn and fabric and set up her studio, announcing that she was going back to her *real* work. She took breaks only to do food shopping and to cook for them. Nick and Brendan got stuck with washing dishes.

The whole downstairs had begun to have a comfortable, lived-in appearance, reminding Brendan of their old apartment. Heaps of books and magazines were sprouting in lopsided growths on chairs and end tables. Bits of yarn clung to the small carpet in the hallway. Only their father's chair escaped the creeping disorder that always accompanied their mother's creation of a new wall hanging. The chair sat empty amid the confusion.

As the rainy days slumped along, Ami stayed in her room with the door shut. No sound escaped. It was as if she were sealing herself up. Brendan imagined her wrapped in blankets like a cocoon and then emerging transformed. Yet each time their mother coaxed her out for a brief meal, she was just the same—picking at her food and acting sullen. Once she left her door ajar when she went to the bathroom, and Brendan, who had gone upstairs to get a puzzle, peeked into her bedroom. The shades were drawn all the way down, but he could see a pile of books next to her jumbled bed, and he wondered if she was doing more research on unicorns. Her bureau was crowded with her unicorn collection, and on top of her large desk, a circular arrangement of candles flickered. They cast eerie patterns of light against the yellow walls. He remembered Ami dancing around in a circle in the dark yard and wondered if she'd let those fireflies loose. They could still be in her room, probably suffocated in that stupid jar. When he heard the toilet flush, he tiptoed quickly away.

On the fifth day of wet weather, Brendan wandered aimlessly into the studio and stood next to the table, watching his mother. He found it comforting to see her in a familiar pose, chin cupped in her hand, eyes narrowed as she arranged and rearranged her materials on the large table.

Another wall patch. The thought gave him a sense of satisfaction. Mom had often told them the story about her very first wall patch. When she and Dad had gotten married, they'd lived in a tiny fourth-floor walk-up apartment in Brooklyn. Their walls had been scruffy and cracked. Mom had covered up a small hole with one of her fabric-and-handwoven pieces from art school. "A wall patch," she'd called it. She'd made others, each to cover a specific deformity of their walls. Soon she was making more for people to hang on perfect surfaces, but the name "wall patch" had stuck.

Now Mom looked up and smiled. Brendan studied the pattern made of fabric scraps and the small pencil sketch she'd done on paper. "I like it," he said.

Nick came into the room, chomping on an apple. "Where're you going to sell it, Mom? You really think there's a market for original stuff way out here in the sticks?"

"Not to worry. I've got some work to do on commission left over from New York. And besides, I'll be teaching three classes at the community college in the fall, remember? You won't starve, Nicholas. I promise! We have no mortgage on this place and no rent."

Brendan followed Nick back into the living room, where they were watching a baseball game. The players seemed to be moving in slow motion. It was as boring as old comedy reruns, but at least it didn't take much concentration to watch. Since the rain had started, they had finished reading all their library books and put together half a dozen puzzles. The day before, they had begun to build sophisticated machines, trying to use up every Lego in their collection. Only two half-full shoeboxes remained, but it was getting more difficult. Most of the good pieces had already been used to build the four spaceships, lunar lander, aircraft carrier, six racecars, futuristic tank, and multipurpose vehicle. Brendan had just located a wheel he'd been looking for when the jangle of the phone made his hand jerk.

"I'll get it!" yelled Nick as he dashed into the kitchen. It was a well-formed habit to answer the phone whenever their mother was creating. Before Brendan could get up hopes that the call was about Shag, Nick yelled, "Ami! For you."

She took her time coming to the phone. Her footsteps on the winding stairs sounded like slurred speech—as if she were still half asleep and her feet mumbling.

Nick called impatiently, "Hurry up!" He held the phone out into the hallway with the cord stretched taut.

"Shut up." She grabbed the receiver, said a sullen hello, then scuffed into the kitchen.

"It's that guy we saw at Swallow Hole. Jonny's big brother," Nick told Brendan. They tried to listen to Ami's side of the conversation, but her voice was too low.

When she hung up a minute later and started for the stairs, their mother came out of the studio and asked, her voice sounding artificially casual, "Who was that, Ami?"

"Some guy."

"A friend from New York?"

"No, Mom." She spoke with exaggerated patience, as if their mother were not very bright. "It was some country jerk who wanted me to go out with him."

"Oh, well, I don't think . . . But he's welcome to come here. . . ."

"Mom! Stop it! I'm not *going,* and he's not *coming.* Leave me alone!"

"Good grief, Ami, I wasn't . . . I just thought it'd be nice for you to spend some time with other young people."

"Oh, forget it, Mom. If I get any more phone calls, just tell them I'm *dead.*"

Nick made a snort of disgust. "Stop being melodramatic."

"Leave me alone, you jerk!" Ami scowled at him, then flounced away. Brendan noticed that her tangled hair looked stringy and neglected.

Their mother stood still for a moment as Ami disappeared back upstairs. Then she turned toward the boys. Above her glasses, her brow was wrinkled, and she blinked twice before saying softly, "Maybe she just . . . misses her old friends or . . ." Her voice trailed away as she returned to her studio.

Brendan stared at the remaining Legos. His stomach felt as if he'd eaten too much of something sour, like pickles.

"I need the piece to make the propellers turn," Nick said, pointing to the space at the top of the helicopter he was making.

"Strike three," said the television, and another player slouched his way to the bench.

"Here." Brendan found the Lego part and handed it to Nick.

They worked silently, not really listening to the ball game or the clinking of the small plastic blocks as they searched for the right pieces.

Finally, the game ended, and they only had odd, spare Legos left.

"What can we make out of these?" Nick asked, shaking the two shoeboxes.

Brendan said, "Maybe we could fit them onto the things we've already made."

"Nah. Those things are perfect now. 'Sides, that would be sort of cheating."

Brendan agreed. So, feeling defeated, they dumped the pieces together into the smaller box. Later Brendan shoved it under his bed. Out of sight.

That night it stopped raining and turned cooler. When Brendan went upstairs, he tossed an extra blanket on his bed. On his way to the bathroom, he heard soft murmurs coming from Ami's room. Stepping quietly and holding his breath, he listened by her door. She seemed to be talking to someone in a coaxing, gentle voice. Although he couldn't make out her words, he knew that she was pretending to talk to the unicorn. Practicing for the day when she captures it, he thought. Brendan shivered.

When he got back to his own room, he wished that Nick would come in and talk. But Nick had his radio tuned to a staticky station and hadn't even bothered to say good night. In the mirror on the back of his door, Brendan glanced at his reflection. He remembered when he and Nick had been about four years old and had looked at themselves in a department store three-piece mirror. Each huge section had extended far above their heads, and at first it had been fun, making faces, jumping around, seeing themselves repeated and repeated. But then Brendan had realized that he wasn't sure which one of those reflected boys was himself.

At some point during the night, Brendan awoke. Gently, he moved Shere Khan off his stomach, then got up and crossed the room to look out his back window. He sank down and sat cross-legged on the floor, resting his hands on the rough paint of the window sill. The scene looked mysterious, and he blinked. His eyes adjusted slowly to the faint moonlight. The leaves of the tree next to the house looked as if they'd been brushed with diluted silver paint. Beyond the over-grown backyard, meadow grasses swayed in a dark breeze, and distant trees cast elongated shadows. Night insects hummed incessantly.

The moon appeared to have been sliced in half, but of course, that wasn't true. One chilly night on a camping trip, Dad had explained the phases of the moon. The whole concept had sounded wonderfully scientific and yet almost magical. Now Brendan took a deep breath and tasted the cool, rain-washed air, so different from the sultry heat of the week before.

For a long time, he sat and looked outside. No sign of Ami. Good! He stifled a yawn and stretched his legs. Nothing was happening out there, so he might as well get back into bed. As Brendan started to stand up, he noticed something different in the night landscape. He slid back to his knees and stared.

At the edge of the meadow, where the denseness of the woods swallowed the thin moonlight, one shadow was moving, detaching itself from the trees. It looked like an animal. A dog? No, too big. A deer maybe? No, still too big. A cow? Could be. *A unicorn?*

Brendan didn't dare take his eyes from that shape for fear he'd lose it—as if his gaze were holding it in place. But finally he blinked, and when he searched, almost frantically, for the shadowy figure again, it was gone, melted back into the general dark of the woods. He sighed, feeling a strange mixture of regret and relief.

Chapter Ten

As soon as Brendan opened his eyes, he realized he'd slept late. He staggered up and tripped over his blanket, which had fallen in a heap on the floor. If Shag had been here, she would have wakened him earlier with a warm lick. Shere Khan simply glanced up at him from his nest at the foot of the bed.

When Brendan went downstairs, he found Nick gulping orange juice out of the carton and Ami sitting at the kitchen table stirring yogurt around in its container.

"Is that you, Brendan?" called Mom from her studio. "Welcome to a perfect day, sleepyhead. No rain! Pure unadulterated sunshine pouring down."

"Let's do some more exploring today," suggested Nick as Brendan slurped cold cereal. "Or maybe go fishing. I bet those trailer kids know some good fishing spots."

"We hate fishing!" said Brendan. Camping trips had never included fishing.

"Yeah," Nick said. "But isn't that what country kids do? I mean 'sides swimming and hiking. Or maybe we should just get on our bikes and go find the trailer where those kids live. I bet they've got a VCR that works."

"Picnics," said Ami. Brendan glanced at her with surprise. Not only had she emerged from her room, she was joining in a conversation.

"Huh?" Nick wrinkled his nose.

"Picnics. That's a country thing. Let's make a picnic lunch and go for a hike and eat."

Brendan looked at Ami suspiciously. "You don't eat, remember?"

"I do too. Just 'cause I don't stuff myself like you two pigs doesn't mean I don't eat. Besides, a picnic is different."

Nick shrugged and said, "Anything that involves food sounds good to me. Let's invite Jonny. He made me memorize his phone number when we were at the pool."

Ami nodded agreeably. "Sure, ask him along, why not?"

After Nick made the phone call, he reported that Jonny would skip the picnic. His mom was making her special lasagna for lunch. But he'd meet them near the pool in about two hours. Nick joined Ami and Brendan as they rummaged through the cupboards, pulling out cans and jars and boxes. They put pineapple, pickles, and raisins in plastic bags and made peanut butter and jelly sandwiches. Brendan licked the knife one time too many; his stomach growled in protest.

"We need another sandwich," said Nick. "That'll make two each."

Mom came into the kitchen to pour herself a cup of

coffee. She smiled at the bustle of activity. "A picnic? Sounds lovely. You three have fun," she said as she went back into her studio.

"I made a list." Ami shook open a large paper bag.

"We don't need a list. We've got everything we need right here." Nick pointed to the stack of sandwiches and heap of other food.

"No, stupid. A list—well, actually a plan. For catching the unicorn."

"Ami, cut it out." Nick grabbed the bag from her and began to jam sandwiches into it.

"I'm all organized," she continued as if he hadn't said a word. "See?" Pulling a sheet of folded paper from her jeans pocket, she smoothed it out on the table.

Brendan was impressed. At the top, Ami had drawn a dark unicorn head with tangled forelock and dilated nostrils. She'd shaded the horn to make it look twisted.

"I never heard of a black unicorn," said Nick skeptically.

"So? Who cares? This one's black." Ami sounded certain.

The list was printed in graceful calligraphy and started with number one: Look for more prints around Swallow Hole. And ended with number ten: Bring unicorn home.

"What's that number three?" asked Nick. "Who exactly is going to help you build a unicorn lure? Whatever *that* is." Brendan wondered, too. He didn't recall reading anything about lures in Ami's notebook. She was probably making up her own unicorn myths by now.

"You'll see," said Ami.

"Aren't you a little too old for this make-believe stuff?" Nick asked.

"You don't know what you're talking about, Nicholas. Just shut up. If you don't want to come, stay home and play with your infantile baseball cards, Legos, or whatever."

"Baseball cards make sense, Ami. You don't!"

Brendan was looking at the map that Ami had drawn at the bottom of the page. "I think the trailer court is closer to Swallow Hole than you've got it," he said. "And you completely forgot the place way up in the hills where that insane old geezer lives."

"Shut up! You two can be so infuriating!" Ami snatched up the plan and shoved it back into her pocket. "That stuff isn't important. The woods are what matter. Unicorns are shy, sylvan creatures. They live in the *forest*."

Nick grunted. "I bet this one lives in some weirdo's head." Ami scowled at him.

"It's like one of those stories," Brendan said, suddenly wanting to keep things from escalating into a no-win argument. "Like one that . . . Dad made up. Like our dwarf story, Nick. It could be fun, you know. Just pretending."

"Yeah," Nick said grudgingly. *"Pretending."*

"Whatever," Ami muttered between her teeth.

"Maybe we should split up the food," suggested Brendan quickly. He wanted to get to the woods and play a game of pretend the way they used to do when Dad was alive. When things were safe and fun. "Put it in three bags instead of one big one. Looks kind of heavy, and who's going to carry it?"

93

"We'll take turns," said Ami as she thrust the last sandwich into the bag.

Sure, thought Brendan without conviction. But he gave Nick a look that said, Don't mess with her. It's not worth it.

He and Nick waited while Ami went upstairs and came back down with a bulging backpack. "What've you got in there?" asked Nick.

"You'll see when it's time," Ami said mysteriously.

Nick just shrugged. They left their mother working in her studio and, by unspoken agreement, headed toward the brook. Brendan carried the paper bag against his body as he lunged awkwardly from rock to rock. Since the rain, the water was much deeper, and the dry surfaces at the tops of rocks had shrunk or disappeared altogether.

After a reasonable length of time, Nick took the bag and carried it until they could hear the falls. Then he called to Ami, who had gotten a short distance ahead. "Hey, wait up." He held the bag aloft. "Your turn!"

"I can't. I'll fall. My balance isn't as good as you guys'. And my backpack is so heavy!"

"Oh, sure, Ami. You promised we'd take turns. You didn't have to bring your dumb backpack."

"I didn't *promise*. But I will carry the bag all the way back," said Ami.

"What? You think we're still five years old and will fall for that kind of trick? No way! Here! Take it!" Nick heaved the bag toward Ami. She was teetering on a rock. Instead of trying to catch it, she flung up her hands to protect her face. The bag tumbled into the water.

They all stood on their respective rocks and watched their lunch get buffeted and begin to list to one side, but it was still afloat.

"Now look what you've done!" yelled Ami.

"*Me?*" Nick managed to sound both furious and injured.

Brendan stepped off his rock cautiously. It took just a moment for the cold water to soak through his jeans and hit his legs with a pang that gave his heart a jolt. It was much deeper than he'd expected, coming above his knees immediately and even higher as he waded out toward the partially submerged bag. He wasn't sure whether it would sink or be swept along with the water.

"Forget it!" screamed Ami. "Everything's ruined now."

Despite Ami's protest, Brendan persisted, wading with the current, surprised at how strong it was. The rain-swollen brook moved with purpose—heading for the waterfall—churning up against the rocks where branches and weeds were snagged, and snatching at them until they washed on, only to get caught on the next rock or the next.

Brendan kept his eyes on the bag, feeling with his sneakered feet along the rocky bottom. One more step. He reached forward with both hands. The bag had gotten wedged against an underwater rock. If he stretched . . .

His left foot slipped, and he fell. *Splat!* Brendan went completely under the water. The current grabbed him, pulling and sucking as if it had been waiting for him to make one wrong move. He fought back. The water was a bully, shoving and thumping him against a rock as his lungs burned for air. *Where's the surface? Which way is up?* he screamed silently. Panic made him flail his arms and scrape his knuckles on a rough rock. He grabbed for it, inching his hands and body up toward air. Finally, Brendan was standing again, his head and torso above water.

As he shook his wet hair and wiped his eyes, he saw Nick and Ami, doubled over on their rocks, laughing.

Brendan couldn't believe it. They hadn't even noticed that he'd almost drowned. And there was that stupid bag, stuck and sinking fast. He felt a little crazy, as if he had to get it now that he'd already risked his life. He waded closer, ignoring the depth and shoving current. The line of water above his waist felt like a band of frozen wire. He grabbed the bag, using both hands to hold the bottom and one soggy side. The paper was giving way between his fingers, getting ready to deteriorate and spew the contents into the brook. So, with a mighty lift and push, he sent the whole wet mess sailing onto a large rock at the edge.

"Bravo!" shouted Nick. "You look like Shere Khan that time he fell in the tub."

"And now I know just how he felt." Brendan staggered against the rock, dragged himself up over it on his stomach, then rolled to one side and pulled up his wet legs. His sneakers made a squishing sound as he braced his feet against the slope of the rock. Sitting up, he peeled the front of his T-shirt away from his stomach to wring out the water. But there was nothing to do about his drenched jeans. Why hadn't he worn shorts?

"Let's go back," he said angrily. "This picnic idea is stupid." Almost as bad as looking for a nonexistent unicorn, he thought. Or a dead dog.

"You go back," said Ami. "Nick and I can look for tracks."

"But I'm starving," said Nick. He'd gotten to the tattered bag and was digging through it. He held up a sandwich. "See? Not even damp. The wonders of little plastic sandwich bags."

"Let's eat our provisions right here," Ami suggested.

"This is like the Expedition to the North Pole," said Nick cheerfully, referring to the Winnie-the-Pooh story. It had been one their father had read over and over when they were all little. He'd made each animal speak with a distinctive voice.

Ami and Nick clambered about on the rock, arranging themselves and the pile of food. Brendan was quiet, remembering his father's voice squeaking, imitating Roo after he'd fallen into the stream.

Brendan took off his sneakers, dumped the water out of them, and set them in a patch of sunshine. When Ami smiled and offered him a sandwich, he accepted it as a peace token and took a large bite.

Chapter Eleven

While they ate, Brendan's clothing dried, and Ami talked. It seemed as if she'd been hoarding words and now let them pour out like water over the falls. She talked about the unicorn as if it really existed. Brendan found himself imagining the elusive creature moving silently through the woods, or forest, as Ami called it. Nick rolled his eyes when Ami said, "I'm Maid Amelia. My heart is pure, and you two are my helpers in the quest for the unicorn."

"Helpers? What, like some kind of servants?" asked Nick.

"No, dwarves," said Brendan, keeping his tone light. His gaze was drawn by a small twig in the brook as it moved steadily toward the waterfall. "We're these two dwarves that are destined to assist the maiden of pure heart in her search for the unicorn. And . . . there's a mean old ogre who lives on top of the mountain."

"O.K., dwarves and an ogre," Nick said and grinned suddenly. "I like the ogre."

When they were done eating, they continued on to Swallow Hole, where Ami began immediately to walk along the edge, searching for tracks. "I don't see any fresh ones," she announced with a shake of her head.

"Hey, you guys!" Jonny greeted them as he came out of the woods.

"Hi, Ami!" It was Sandy, leaping up on a rock and practically screaming.

"We're playing a game, sort of," Brendan explained when Ami simply waved distractedly from the other side of the pool and continued staring at the ground. "She's looking for tracks. Our dog is still missing. But we have this story that we're acting out."

"About a unicorn," said Nick.

"O.K.!" Ami called, heading toward them. "Let's get started. I have everything we need," she patted her backpack, "but we have to find the correct spot."

"What's she talking about?" Jonny whispered to Nick.

"The story. The unicorn. Who knows? We'll just humor her. It'll be fun. See, Brendan and I are pretending to be these two dwarves, and you can be . . . whatever you want. Have you ever read Tolkien's books? You could maybe be a hobbit or something."

Jonny shook his head, looking baffled.

"How about the Narnia tales?" asked Brendan. "*The Lion, the Witch and the Wardrobe?*"

"I know that story!" Sandy said, nodding enthusiastically. "I think I seen it on TV."

"Well, maybe." Ami had joined them. "But this is different. This is our *own* secret world here in the dark forest. Our own place. We just have to locate the exact spot to build a unicorn lure."

"If they're dwarves, who are you?" Sandy cocked her head to one side as she studied Ami.

"I'm Maid Amelia. And you can be . . . you can be an elf maiden. Would you like that?"

"Can I name myself?" Sandy asked. "I want to be called Acetaminophen."

"What?" Jonny began to laugh. "That's the name of some pills for headaches, stupid."

"I don't care!" Sandy sounded close to tears. She whacked at her brother with her small hands, but Jonny dodged out of her reach.

"Acetaminophen is a lovely name," said Ami quickly. "Follow me." She led them away from the pool, downstream and then into the woods. She kept glancing up and soon stopped. In a hushed, reverent voice, Ami said, "This is it. This is the correct tree." She placed her hands on the smooth, gray bark of a tall trunk that looked, to Brendan, much like the others surrounding it. Next Ami shrugged off her backpack and dug inside a pocket. "Here's a carving instrument," she said as she held up an old screwdriver. "We shall use it to engrave our symbols in the bark. We shall take turns while the others collect the required rocks."

"What kind of rocks?" asked Nick. "Not heavy ones, I hope."

"What's my symbol?" asked Sandy, squinting up at Ami earnestly.

"Acetaminophen, your symbol is a circle," Ami said.

"Yeah, like a pill, you get it?" Jonny chuckled, and Sandy frowned.

"No." Ami's voice was authoritative. "It is a circle

like the full moon. Only during the full moon can a unicorn be captured. So Acetaminophen's symbol is very special. And significant."

"See? I'm sing . . . sig . . . Whatever she said." Sandy smiled.

"How come she can say 'acetaminophen' but not other big words?" asked Nick as if Sandy weren't standing right there. She stuck out her tongue at him.

"'Cause our mom's a nurse," explained Jonny. "We've been hearing words like that forever. If we had a normal mom, Sandy would probably want to have an elf name of Tylenol."

"Quit talking about me!" Sandy yelled loudly as if her voice could make up for her size.

"Silence!" Ami said fiercely. "This is no time for frivolous arguments. Here, I will bestow upon each of you an assigned symbol. Remember them." She dug a pad of paper and a stubby pencil from her backpack and drew a circle.

"I already know how to make a circle," said Sandy, sounding offended. "I'm not stupid."

"Elf Acetaminophen, do you wish to participate or to leave the Unicorn Tree and never return?" asked Maid Amelia in her superior tone.

"No way. I'm in," said Acetaminophen with a solemn nod.

Jonny's symbol was a star, and Nick's a zigzag of lightning. Brendan watched as Ami drew another lightning bolt for his symbol, identical to Nick's. But when she handed it to him, he realized that no, they were not exactly alike. They were mirror images of each other.

101

He swallowed and stared at Ami, wondering if she thought he was just some sort of reflection of Nick.

But she continued to talk in her Maid Amelia voice. "It is necessary that we gather the proper rocks. They should be approximately this big." She made a circle with her arms, enclosing a space about a foot across. "And the color must be as dark as possible."

Brendan thought it was fun scrambling through the woods, over logs and around trees, searching for just the right rocks, not too big, not too small, not too light in color. But after he'd lugged four of them to the tree trunk, his arms began to ache, and the sweat on his face attracted insects that buzzed ominously past his ears. Ami stayed by the tree to carve her symbol, a shape like three licks of flame.

As they each returned with their burdens, Ami stopped carving and helped position the rocks in a ring approximately three feet from the tree trunk. "Excellent choice," she told Brendan when he came back with his fifth rock. He felt foolishly pleased that she approved. There was something almost hypnotic about Ami's direction of the group. Even Nick, who was the most skeptical all along, seemed to be enjoying the rock collecting. Brendan noticed that his brother was competing with Jonny to see which of them could find—and carry back alone—the largest rocks.

Sandy's rocks were all small and too pale, according to Ami, who generously told the younger girl that these could be used as part of the path that they would soon make leading from the tree to the stream. "So the unicorn will follow it and come right to this tree. Here he will lay his head down to rest; here he will become part of our world."

What an imagination, thought Brendan.

"When can we make the path?" asked Sandy, dropping a rock so close to Brendan's foot that he had to leap out of the way.

"Maybe tomorrow. Now I've finished my symbol. You want me to help you make your circle, Acetaminophen?"

"I can do it myself." Sandy bit her lower lip in concentration as she grasped the screwdriver.

"You'd better not cut yourself," Jonny warned.

"I'm not a baby!" But the circle Sandy carved looked more like a jagged hexagon.

Brendan wanted to make his lightning bolt before Nick made his, but when he staggered back with his seventh rock, Nick had already gouged his symbol into the tree.

"Here, your turn," Nick said, tossing the screwdriver to him. Brendan caught it and set to work. The bark gave way beneath the sharp edge of the tool. He dug deeper and wider than Nick had, feeling a certain satisfaction that his symbol would be more visible.

Ami stood on one of the larger rocks that Jonny had lugged to the site. "We have accomplished much today," she said, smiling kindly on her subjects. "Next, we will scout the stream that descends from the mountain. We will search for a perfect spot for another unicorn lure."

"What? Another one?" Nick spat in disgust. "Get real, Ami."

She continued as if she hadn't heard him. "Three is

the magic number. We need to construct three lures in order to entice the unicorn."

"What stream are you talking about?" asked Jonny, wiping his nose on his bare arm. "Not that little one that comes down into Swallow Hole?"

"Yes, precisely that one," said Ami.

"No way. Count me out." Jonny shook his head emphatically.

"That's Old Man Johansson's mountain," said Sandy, her eyes wide. "You aren't going to make us go up *there,* are you, Maid Amelia? He'll kill anybody that comes up close to his house. He hates tres . . . trespassers!"

"I thought you said that he owned Swallow Hole," said Nick, frowning. "He doesn't seem to mind everybody swimming there."

Jonny shook his head. "That's just because he doesn't know we're there."

Ami folded her arms and stared straight ahead, out above them into the forest. "You may leave, Hobbit Jon and Elf Acetaminophen. We no longer are in need of your assistance."

"Ah, please," Sandy begged. "We can make more unicorn lures right around here. We don't have to go way up there, Maid Amelia."

Ami was stone-faced. "Depart. Leave. Go." She pointed in the direction of the path to the trailer court.

"Shoot," Sandy said, looking close to tears. "I want to stay. You can't tell me what to do."

"But *I* can," said Jonny. "You know Mom doesn't want us going anywhere near that crazy man's place. Sorry, you guys, we're leaving." He grabbed Sandy's hand and dragged her away, stumbling and protesting.

Chapter Twelve

After the noise of Jonny and Sandy's departure died down, there was silence. Ami stood on the rock with a blank, calm expression on her face.

Nick whacked a stick against a tree trunk. "Why'd you have to go and make Jonny leave, Ami? Just when we were having fun. Let's go home."

"Not yet." Ami hopped down and pulled something out of her backpack. It was wrapped in toilet paper. As she unwound it, Brendan and Nick watched. In a moment, a tiny glass unicorn emerged. Ami shoved the mass of tissue into her backpack with one hand, holding the unicorn aloft with the other. "This is the image of the unicorn, placed here in this sacred lure to welcome the living creature," she said in her high-pitched Maid Amelia voice. As she spoke, she carefully set the tiny statue on top of one nearly level rock. "I am in need of three identical leaves," she said, turning toward the boys.

"Forget leaves. I'm hungry," said Nick.

"You can't possibly be hungry. You just ate enough to kill a pig." Ami's normal big-sister voice was back.

"Here." Brendan grabbed three tiny leaves off a

scraggly bush and handed them to Ami. With a satisfied smile, she placed them around the glass unicorn.

"Now we can depart." She stood, slung her backpack over her shoulder, and dusted off her hands. Then she turned toward Swallow Hole. "Follow Maid Amelia up the tributary."

"Sounds like some sort of geography lesson," muttered Nick as they scurried around the edge of the pool. He raised his voice. "How come we have to go up along *that* stream, Ami? Didn't you hear what Jonny said?"

She stopped to glare. "What's with you guys? You're turning into wimps!"

"We're not wimps! We just have a few brains. This is stupid, right, Brendan?"

Brendan hesitated just long enough for Ami to notice. "See?" she shot back at Nick. "*Brendan* wants to come. He knows it'll be fun. It's all part of the *game,* right, Brendan?"

He didn't know how to respond. Somehow, he felt she was mocking him, setting him up. But he really did want to go up the tributary. He wanted to stay inside the forest. Inside the pretend world that Ami was so good at constructing.

He glanced at Nick. "I . . . I think it'll be O.K."

Nick stared back at him for a moment, then shrugged. "It's no big deal. And I'm not scared of some old dude who lives in a shack in the woods." He grinned. "Hey, I've decided on my dwarf name! I'll be Wimper, and you're Wimpet, O.K.?"

Brendan nodded. They'd learned long ago that this was the easiest way to deal with Ami. When she teased them, they would agree with her when she expected them to disagree. So the two dwarves, Wimper and Wimpet, followed Maid Amelia.

Going up along the thin, fast-moving stream was rough. Brendan grabbed saplings and used them like walking sticks to heave himself over rocks that crowded close to the water. His bare feet slid and rubbed in his damp sneakers. He was sure he'd have a blister soon.

Inside his head, Brendan could hear the story playing out. *We are twin dwarves, venturing into the depths of the forest. The bubbling stream is a magic thread, leading us up the mountain.*

The air was filled with a rich scent of damp vegetation. They climbed on and on, and Brendan lost all sense of time and distance. He noticed that Ami was no longer searching for a spot for another unicorn lure, but he didn't care.

"Hey!" Ami stopped and leaned forward, her face close to the water. "Another hoofprint. I knew the unicorn would be up here someplace."

Brendan stared off into the woods to where the green turned darker. He remembered the shadow in the moonlight that he had seen the night before, but he said nothing. He blinked, thinking of animals beyond his vision, blending into the trunks and leaves. Like one of those "hidden pictures" in a kiddie magazine. Take your red crayon and circle the cat, fox, deer . . . and unicorn.

Kneeling beside Ami, Nick said, "It's not very clear. Maybe it's a deer track. But look, here's one from a fox or something."

"Shag!" Ami's voice was shrill.

"No, too small for Shag," Nick said sadly. "Besides, you're the one who says she's dead, Ami."

"It could be Shag's," said Ami stubbornly, ignoring Nick. "Shag! Here, Shag!"

No sound, not even an echo answered her call. Brendan felt a hollow space somewhere inside and remembered waking one dark night shortly after their father had died. Nick, in the bed across the room, was calling hoarsely in his sleep, "Daddy! Daddy!" For just a moment, in his half-conscious state, Brendan had expected to hear Dad's voice. "Coming, son." But then Brendan had remembered.

Now, here in the woods, Ami yelled again. "Shag! Here, girl!" She put her two fingers between her lips and gave the earsplitting whistle that had always sent Shag into a yelping frenzy. Dad had taught her how to do that whistle.

"Stop it!" Nick said angrily. "Think! She's dead. It's been two weeks since she ran away."

What was that? A faint staccato sound in the distance.

"Quiet!" said Ami. "Listen. That's a dog. For sure. Let's go, fathead."

"What a sweet mouth on Maid Amelia," Nick said sarcastically, then added, "It can't be Shag." But he took off after Ami.

Brendan's heart thudded in his ears as he scrambled along the narrow creek. They all stopped for Ami to whistle again.

Now the answering faint chorus of yelps was off to the left on one side of the creek. They clawed their way up the embankment, around rocks and boulders, and veered into the woods toward the barking. It felt a little scary, leaving the security of the water.

Brendan sensed the building before they reached it—a certain denseness that he thought at first was tree trunks but became the weathered wood of the side of a barn. Saplings and brush grew right against it, and a tangle of poison ivy crept upward and wound around a high, broken window.

They stopped, breathing heavily. From somewhere beyond the barrier, a dog whined plaintively. Ami's normally pale face was flushed. She licked her lips. "Lift me up."

"That's poison ivy!" But Brendan helped Nick hoist Ami toward the opening.

"I can't see. Too high. But I'm sure it's her!" Ami jumped down and added, "Wait here. I'm going to find a door."

Brendan nodded. Out of the corner of his eye, he saw Nick do the same. Ami disappeared around the side of the barn, and they stood, trying to breathe quietly, listening to her progress as she struggled through the dense growth. The dog continued to whine. Brendan felt a stirring of hope. He heard a faint creaking sound, like an old door being opened, and then a brief, happy bark.

The bark was followed almost immediately by someone yelling. Not Ami. It was a man's voice. "Who are you? What are you doing here? Hey, stop! That's *my* dog! Stop or I'll shoot!"

Ami burst through the tangle of weeds. The blast of a shotgun into the treetops jolted Brendan to his toes.

"Run!" Ami screamed. Right behind her was a blur of golden fur.

Shag!

They ran pell-mell through the woods, crashed down the slope, finding the stream more by accident than design. When they could not hear shots or shouts, they slowed and tried to catch their breath. Shag leaped up on Brendan, covering his face and hands with sloppy kisses. It was as if she'd returned from the dead. The joy he felt was so intense, it hurt.

Ami knelt beside the dog, burying her face in Shag's fur. When she looked up, there were tears glistening in her eyes. It seemed to be Maid Amelia speaking when she said, "The unicorn has great powers."

"I'd say Shag has powers of her own. She survived right there in the ogre's lair. What an amazing dog!" Nick rubbed Shag's head, and she looked up at him.

Brendan laughed. "See! She *does* know how to grin!"

Chapter Thirteen

"I don't get it," said Nick. They were walking toward the house from the mailbox, and he was holding Shag's leash. It had been three days since they'd found her, and no one had suggested letting her go free again. But she was content to walk along beside them, snuffling the grassy ridge in the middle of the lane, her tail waving. Every so often, she grinned up at them.

"She loves us now that she's discovered the big, bad woods," said Brendan.

"I wasn't talking about Shag. I meant I don't get it about Ami. How come she started calling for Shag in the woods when *she* was the one so sure Shag was dead?"

Brendan looked at his brother.

"Yeah, O.K.," said Nick. "I know. Nothing Ami does makes sense."

"Right. It's like she's obsessed." It was true. Finding Shag had not diverted Ami's interest from her search for the unicorn. "She came into my room last night," Brendan continued. "I pretended I was too sleepy to talk. She said maybe three unicorn lures won't be necessary. Like we're supposed to rejoice or something. And she went on and on about the powers of light. You know she's got a whole bunch of candles in her room? And she kept talking about the moon. She also said we have to go spy on that place where we found Shag. She's sure the unicorn is up there on that mountain. Says she saw a sign. Whatever *that* means. Maybe another hoofprint."

"Maybe some unicorn poop."

"Yeah." Brendan grinned. But he wished Nick would say something to help him understand his own feelings about Ami's quest. He was finding it appealing in a way that he couldn't figure out.

Nick just grunted in disgust. "I sure don't want to go back there. I guess Jonny wasn't making up all that stuff. That crazy old man actually shot at us!"

"I don't think he was really trying to hit us," Brendan said slowly. He didn't want to think about Old Man Johansson. Instead, he was remembering the shadow that had emerged from the woods the night after the rain. He shook his head as he glanced at the envelopes and papers clutched in his hand. Junk mail, addressed to Current Resident. An envelope with a window— probably a bill. Advertisements for various discount stores. A square, cream-colored envelope addressed to Lisa Rodrick. It didn't look much like a letter, though. Too small.

"What do you think this is, anyhow?" Brendan held the envelope toward Nick.

"A note from Mom's secret admirer," Nick said, peering at it. "That's why it doesn't have a return address. Just that illegible name up in the corner. Starts with a *D*."

Joking around about Mom and another man made Brendan uncomfortable. He shuffled the envelope in with the rest of the mail. He was glad the initial wasn't *L* for that pharmacist's name.

"Hey, race you!" Nick bounded off. Shag pulled out in front, straining against her collar, eager for home.

They ran all the way to the house, up the steps, across the wooden porch, through the living room, and into the studio.

"Whoa! You guys nearly knocked me over!" cried Mom.

"I won!" yelled Nick.

"No, Shag's the champ." Brendan tossed the mail onto the table and jerked Shag's leash from Nick. "Come on, girl. Let's dance." The dog leaped up. Brendan grasped her paws, and the two of them twirled around the table.

"Stop!" said Mom. "You're going to destroy the house. Or at the least—and most important—my studio." But she was smiling, and Brendan knew she shared the same giddy thrill that he felt about having their dog safely home.

Mom glanced through the mail and then held up the cream envelope. "Something from Deirdre."

"Told you that was a *D*," said Nick, and Brendan felt a wash of relief. No secret admirer.

Mom opened the envelope and skimmed the short note. "Deirdre has her own gallery now and wants to know if I'd like to exhibit my work." Shaking her head, she added, "Good grief! She says she'd like whatever wall patches I've got for her grand opening. She needs them by this Thursday!"

"Go for it, Mom," said Nick.

"Thursday? Impossible." Mom shoved her hair behind her ears. "That means I'd have to be ready by Wednesday. Somebody else must have backed out. That's why she's inviting me on such short notice."

"Mom," Brendan said. "Who cares? It'd still be a great chance to show your stuff."

"What stuff? I sold my best piece last Christmas. All I've got are some old things and then this one I'm working on. It's a great opportunity, though. . . ."

"Just do it!" Nick and Brendan said nearly simultaneously.

"But how could I be ready?" She glanced at her watch as if every minute counted.

"Relax, Mom," said Brendan. "We'll help you."

Their mother groaned. "Never mind. I remember the last time you two helped me. You got completely snarled up in my yarn, and I thought you were going to choke yourselves. I actually had to cut it off you."

"But then we were three years old," Nick said. "This time we'll help by staying out of your way and taking care of ourselves. You won't even have to cook for us."

"Peanut butter, here we come," muttered Brendan.

"Two days," Mom whispered as she touched the wall patch she was working on. "Wait, I know what you can do. I want to weave some objects into this one. Things like real twigs and stones. You could go find some for me. I really don't have time now to scout them out myself."

"I know where there're some neat vines. Real scraggly and hairy. You could trim off the leaves. You want them?" asked Nick.

"Well . . ."

"Nick," said Brendan, "you're talking about *poison ivy.*"

"It'd make great interactive art," said Nick. "You know? You could put a sign next to it saying, 'Touch me,' and then have video cameras set up to record the people scratching."

Brendan shook his head. "Poison ivy doesn't work that fast. See, here's that spot on my arm where I touched some leaves a couple of days ago, and it just started to itch this morning."

"Too bad," said Mom cheerfully as she started threading a huge needle with dark green yarn. "Now, scoot, you guys. I need some quiet to work."

Brendan and Nick spent the rest of that day on their own. Mom was busy, and Ami was doing . . . whatever Ami did in her room for hours. First, the boys found some natural materials for their mother's wall patch. After lunch, they located their helmets, both of which had ended up in Nick's closet. Then they dragged their dusty bikes out of the barn where they'd stored them, pumped up the tires, and pedaled down the lane to the main road. Neither of them said a word about this being the first time they'd ridden bikes since their dad's death.

Without discussing their destination, they turned

toward the trailer court. The sun was shining, but the air felt cool, especially in the shade of the trees that leaned over the blacktop road. Their bikes picked up speed on the long downward slope, and Brendan swung his body into the curves, thrilled by the sense of freedom. The line of mailboxes appeared suddenly, and they braked and fishtailed toward the center of the road.

It took a while to locate Jonny's place. They tried to ask an old man who was working on his tiny yard, but he couldn't hear them over the roar of the power mower. The only other people they saw outside were some small children who were digging a trench in one of the gravel roads that crisscrossed the trailer court.

"You guys know a little kid named Sandy?" Nick asked one of them. The boy had a smear of mud across his upper lip that looked like a fake mustache.

"She lives next to the purple ducks." He was right. Several streets over, they found a front lawn decorated with a whole flock of purple wooden ducks. Jonny was home in the beige trailer next-door. His mother introduced herself as Susan Wexler. The boys were mildly relieved to learn that Sandy was at her grandmother's.

"I'm going to take a nap," Mrs. Wexler told them. "You guys are welcome to watch any of the videotapes we've got."

Jonny asked, "Can we play basketball, Mom? We'll be real quiet."

His mother laughed. "I'm so used to the sound of a ball bouncing, it's part of my dreams."

They shot baskets on the patch of driveway next to the trailer. Panda, the black laboodle, bounced with the ball for a while and then lay down under the porch to pant and watch.

"We got our dog back!" Brendan announced.

"Great!" Jonny tossed the basketball, and it slipped through the hoop.

"And we met that old guy up on the mountain," Nick said, dribbling the ball past Jonny.

"Met him?" Jonny nearly tripped over his own feet.

"He was holding our dog captive. He tried to kill us!" Nick was enjoying the drama of the telling. Brendan grinned, even though remembering the sound of that shot made his throat tighten.

But Jonny's reaction was extreme. "Hey!" He stopped and made a time-out signal. "You don't want to mess with that guy. No way. Nohow!"

"Then you're not going to come up there with us when we spy on him?" asked Nick, twirling the ball on his fingertip.

"You're nuts! I didn't tell you before, but when I was real little, that Old Man Johansson came down to Swallow Hole and threatened everybody. Some kids were, you know, throwing beer cans around and writing stuff on the rocks. He cussed them out. But nobody thought he'd really do anything. Then this kid named Carl Moyer, he was found in the water. First everybody thought he'd just drowned. But then they discovered he had a bruise on his head. Maybe he dove in and hit the bottom. But most people think Johansson bashed him and pushed him off a rock."

"So what happened?" asked Nick.

"Nothing. There was no way to prove Johansson

did it. Anyhow, I go swimming at Swallow Hole, but if I hear anybody coming down toward me, I'm outta there. And there's no way . . . none . . . that you'd get me to go up that stupid mountain!"

"Somebody drowned, actually died in that pool?" asked Brendan, goose pimples rising on his arms. He glanced at Nick, who suddenly didn't look nearly so self-assured.

"Yeah, the kid died!" said Jonny. He hesitated, then added, "Still, it's a great place to swim. But, like I say, *nobody* gets me up that mountain."

"Chicken!" Nick had managed to recover and shot the ball at Jonny. "Let's play!"

When they were too hot and sweaty to continue, they went inside and watched a movie, drank can after can of soda, and ate corn curls until their fingers turned bright orange.

Later Mrs. Wexler came back into the living room dressed in a nurse's uniform, ready for second shift at the hospital. "Did I overhear you boys talking about Mr. Johansson?" she asked.

Jonny looked at his fingernails. "I guess. Maybe."

"Well, I just want to remind you of what I've told you before, Jonny. He deserves his privacy. He's had a hard time since his wife died."

"Yeah, he's gone crazy," Jonny muttered.

"No, I don't think so. But people deal with their grief in different ways."

"O.K., Mom, forget it. I'll never go near his place. I swear!"

Talking about Johansson seemed to sour their visit, and

shortly afterward, Nick and Brendan said good-bye and left for home. They were only able to pedal halfway up the hill before the steepness defeated them. Gasping for air, they dismounted to walk the rest of the way.

Early Tuesday night, Mom announced that the wall patch was finished. She had hung it temporarily on the studio wall, and Brendan stared at it for a long time. It was the size of a small window. The material and yarn were all in shades of brown, burnt orange, and green with a touch of pale blue woven throughout that reminded him of the brook. For the top support of the patch, Mom had used a branch he'd found caught between rocks in the rushing water. Its bark was gone. The wood was smooth and bleached to a silvery gray. Three softly rounded stones that Nick had discovered in the backyard were handwoven into the bottom of the wall patch. The whole creation made Brendan think of this place, with its hills, woods, earth, and water. He blinked and realized suddenly that he wanted the wall patch to stay on the wall. And for Mom to stay home.

But she had been busy plucking other wall patches from various locations in the house and digging through several cartons to find more for the art exhibit. Now she stopped in the studio to bite her nails and mutter to herself.

"I like it," Brendan told her, waving a hand toward the newest wall patch. She smiled and went over and took it down. Brendan sighed. It would be babyish to tell Mom he didn't want her to leave. He wandered into the living room and stood next to the couch.

Ami had been maintaining a low profile, but now, the evening before Mom's scheduled departure, she was watching one of those drippy, slow romances made for TV. She looked like she was wearing the same shirt and jeans she'd had on for several days. She had her bare feet propped up on the coffee table. Her soles were dark with grime. Brendan decided not to sit next to her.

"Where's Nick?" he asked.

Ami grunted something unintelligible, then added, "Who cares?"

"Me, or I wouldn't have asked," he said.

"I thought you two always knew where the other one was. You know, the wonderful twin bit," said Ami sarcastically.

"You're right. I must have forgotten we were twins."

As Brendan turned to leave the room, Ami said, "Nick's upstairs sorting his baseball cards or something stupid like that."

"I knew that all along." He ducked as Ami hurled a book at him.

Since Nick was busy, Brendan went back into the studio and found the floor now covered with wall patches. Khan was curled up on one that was made of particularly soft material. Mom was looking at her creations with a critical eye.

"Oh, I completely forgot the patch hanging in the upstairs hallway." She frowned. "My mind is turning to mush. And my finger hurts where I accidentally poked it with the needle."

"Mom, I'll get the one out of the hall. Go soak your injury." When he returned with the wall patch, she was still standing in the same spot, sucking her finger and looking distraught.

"I can't believe it. I forgot all about a sitter. I just can't go!"

"A sitter? Ah, Mom, we don't need one. We're old! We don't need a baby-sitter!"

She shook her head. "It's not for you. I mean, I'm sure you'd all do fine on your own. But I'd be worried sick. I wouldn't enjoy myself at all."

"Jeez, Ami's fourteen—old enough to have her own kid. And we're twelve!"

Mom nervously shoved her hair behind her ears, obviously not listening. "Wait. Maybe there is a way. Brendan, would you start to clean up in here? I've got to make a call."

He found a paper bag and went around the room gathering up scraps of material and yarn. When his mother returned, she looked relieved. "I think it'll be O.K. He was really sweet. Said he was sure his aunt could do it, even at the last minute. She's going to call me in about half an hour."

"Whose aunt?"

"Mr. Latchall's, the pharmacist's."

"The pharmacist? Mom, why'd you call him?" Brendan realized his voice squeaked.

She looked at him distractedly. "Well . . . he's about the only person I've talked to since we moved in whose name I could remember. It was easy to find the number of the pharmacy in the phone book." She began to pile wall patches neatly on the table. "I've got to find that big, flat box."

"Mom," Brendan scratched angrily at the patch of poison ivy on his arm, "what about this lady?" Now a mosquito bite on his neck began to itch, and he dug at that, too.

"Ten, I've got ten pieces altogether. That way, if Deirdre doesn't like a couple of them, I'll still have enough. I can't believe she's invited me. We weren't even very good friends. But I'll be staying with Maria, and I've really missed her and Pierre."

"Mom! The sitter. What's her name, at least?"

"Uh . . . let me think. Mrs. Phillips. Or Phelps. Something with the letters *ph*, I think. As I said, she's his aunt. I met her at the pharmacy the other day when I was there. She seemed nice. Mr. Latchall said she does housecleaning for people sometimes and would be happy to come. She's an older woman. I much prefer that to some crazy teenager."

"Right," Brendan mumbled to himself. "We've already got one of those."

Chapter Fourteen

Early the next morning, Brendan and Nick helped their mother load the car. Ami came downstairs just as they were finishing. She watched for a few minutes with an indifferent expression, then yawned and grumbled something about needing to go back to bed.

"Go!" said Nick with a scowl. "You're no help anyhow."

"Please, don't bicker." Mom looked tired. Her hair was still damp from washing, and loose tendrils curled around her face. After hugs, good-byes, and be-goods, she drove down the narrow lane. They were alone until Old Ph. arrived at noon.

She was a blue-haired woman with eyes to match, and her name was Mrs. Peterman. But Brendan continued to think of her as Old Ph. She didn't seem particularly thrilled about being a baby-sitter for three large children and within a few minutes had tuned the television to her favorite soap and left them to their own devices.

The day was slow and hot. Shag lay in a corner of the kitchen, panting, and Shere Khan stretched out to his fullest length right next to the cellar door in a slight draft of cool air.

123

With Old Ph. monopolizing the TV, they avoided the living room. Brendan suggested a card game, but Nick just shrugged and yawned. Ami had already retreated to her room. Brendan tried to read a magazine, but his eyes kept going shut. Then he decided to take a nap, but there was no air moving across his bed, and he had to keep fanning himself with a sheet of paper, which kept him awake. In the middle of the afternoon, Nick slouched into Brendan's room and invited him to a joint raid on the refrigerator.

They found some cold pizza and flat root beer. Nick began digging in the food cupboard just as Ami wafted into the room. She wore a gigantic, floral-printed scarf draped around her narrow shoulders. Her freshly washed hair flowed down her back like a golden waterfall. On one side of her head, she'd pinned a sprig of some wilted wildflower. Ami twirled around once in the middle of the floor, her scarf, her hair swinging out in a blur of bright colors. The cloying scent of perfume made Brendan almost gag, but he couldn't help thinking of a beautiful moth emerging from its cocoon. Then she fluttered to a stop and announced with startling intensity, "This is our chance. While Mom's gone. And the moon is full with magic."

"What?" said Nick. He was reaching into the bottom of a bag of store-bought sugar cookies.

"It's empty," Brendan told him. "I ate the last one."

"Thanks a lot. You know I love these things." Nick licked crumbs off his fingers.

"Tonight," Ami said as if she had not heard them, "we'll spend the whole night spying at the old man's place. And the unicorn will be mine." She wore a faintly satisfied smile.

Nick shook his head. "No thanks."

"Yes!" She twirled and stopped to face them; her blue eyes glittered. "It is time to complete the quest. It's not mere coincidence that we now have this opportunity. We are being shown the way by the light of the full moon. It is time!"

"Wake up, Maid Amelia," said Nick. "*There is no unicorn!* I'm getting tired of this silly game." He yawned.

"You think it's a game?" Ami asked in her normal voice. "Like what? Monopoly? Or some 'let's pretend' story? No, it's *not* a game. But you two immature dopes don't even know what I'm talking about, do you?" She stared at them, and her lips were drawn thin and taut as if she had more words trapped inside.

But if it's not a game . . . Brendan refused to let his mind go any farther.

"Ah, Ami, stuff it, will you?" Nick crumpled the empty cookie bag and tossed it in the trash. "That old man is nuts, you know. He'll probably shoot us if we come snooping around on his property again."

"There is always danger in a quest," said Ami. "I'll go alone, if need be." With a toss of her head and a swish of colors, she left the kitchen.

"'If need be,'" Nick mimicked. "I hope she gets eaten by the ogre! Talk about indigestion!"

Brendan shrugged. "I don't know. I was sort of looking forward to an adventure. Old Ph. is probably going to make us stay home tomorrow. Maybe tonight's our only chance to have some fun. You know what I'm saying?"

"Yeah." Nick nodded thoughtfully. "Besides, Ami's set us up. She knows we don't want her to go traipsing through the 'forest'—as she insists on calling it—without us. Hey, we might as well make the best of it, right?" Nick opened the refrigerator again and yanked out a pitcher of orange juice. "Let's start planning how to defeat the ogre."

"O.K. We'll need some weapons and a couple of magic spells."

"Food," said Nick. "That'll be our weapon. We'll take some dry Jell-O, and we'll say it's poison, but only for ogres. That way, if the mean old ogre never shows his ugly face, we can always eat the stuff."

Brendan laughed. They shoved packages of lemon and raspberry Jell-O in their pockets, then spent the rest of the afternoon walking Shag and discussing weapons and magic spells. Mrs. Peterman left the television long enough to make fried chicken and mashed potatoes with gravy for dinner. She didn't seem to notice that she had neglected several of the food groups. Just as Brendan was licking the grease off his last finger, the phone rang.

It was their mother, calling from Maria's apartment in Manhattan. Ami talked first, sounding deceptively normal, just making her usual grunts and short answers. Nick babbled about how hot it was. And how they needed to get some more fans. And what time exactly was Mom coming back on Friday, or was it Saturday? And, yes, they were all fine. Yes, all of them.

When it was his turn to talk with her, Brendan was surprised at how she sounded—excited, almost happy.

He wanted to tell her about Ami. *She's come out of her cocoon, Mom. But I don't understand what she's become. Maid Amelia, I guess. And she wants us to go with her on her quest for the unicorn.* But instead he just listened, remembering that day when his mother had said he was the ears. By the time he hung up, his left ear felt warm and tingly.

Ami offered to wash the dishes. Mrs. Peterman ordered the boys to dry and warned them not to go outside again because it would be dark soon. Next she suggested that someone clean the cat's litter pan. Then she went back to the TV to watch a miniseries based on fact about some man who'd had three wives all living in New Jersey.

As Ami ran scalding water into the dishpan, she outlined her plan for the evening. "I'm leaving at around eleven-thirty, as soon as Mrs. Peterman conks out. Are you two coming, or what?"

Nick nodded, and Brendan felt himself do the same. But he realized that he wasn't simply reflecting Nick's decision. *I really want to go with Maid Amelia!* This thought came from some hidden place deep inside him.

Ami was chattering on, sounding nothing like Maid Amelia and exactly like his bossy older sister. "I'm willing to bet Mrs. Peterman'll go up to bed when that inane show's over. She'll take out her false teeth, say her prayers, and go right to sleep."

"Does she really have false teeth?" asked Nick.

Ami was scooping up fistfuls of soapsuds and blowing at them, but she stopped to give Nick a withering look. "That's irrelevant."

"Then why'd you mention it?" asked Nick.

Ami washed and rinsed a knife, then shoved it into the dish rack with a jumble of forks and spoons. As Brendan picked it up, he felt a prickling along his spine. He could imagine the knife jabbing into his skin. He dried the blade gingerly and put it in the drawer, out of sight.

Shere Khan sauntered into the kitchen and gave a demanding cry. "Uh-oh. We forgot to feed him and Shag." Brendan tossed his towel on the table, pleased to have a more enjoyable chore.

Later, as fireflies blinked and drifted from the long grass, Ami announced to Mrs. Peterman, "We're going to go to bed now. Would you like me to take a fan up to your bedroom and put it in your window? That'll make it nice and cool for sleeping."

"That's very thoughtful of you, dear." Mrs. Peterman nodded without shifting her gaze from the television.

As they clumped up the winding stairs, Ami said, "She'll never hear a thing with the fan buzzing away." In the hallway, outside Brendan's door, she stopped and added, "Get your stuff ready right now. Make sure you roll your sleeping bags real tight so they're easy to carry. I've already packed an old plastic jug with juice and some crackers and a bunch of apples for the unicorn."

"What about some candy bars to keep up our energy," suggested Nick.

"Good idea," said Brendan. "You got some?"

"Nah. I thought Ami here was the provider on this expedition."

"We do not need candy," Ami said severely. "This is a stakeout, not a pig-out. When we leave, make sure your beds look as if you're still in them. Make dummies out of some of the junk in your closets—toys, clothes, whatever. There's always a chance Mrs. Peterman'll make at least one bed check."

"Thought you said she'd go right to sleep after she put her teeth in a cup and said her prayers," grumbled Nick.

"I'm just being careful. And I'd advise you to be careful, too. If Mom finds out . . ."

Brendan swallowed. He didn't want to think about Mom at all right now.

Ami continued in a low voice, "I'll knock on your doors three times to signal the all clear. Then we'll go out through Brendan's window 'cause he's got the porch roof and the tree. That way, she won't hear us on the stairs."

"You have a flashlight, right?" asked Nick.

"Yeah, sure."

Inside his room, Brendan worked quickly. He spread his sleeping bag on the floor, then rolled and tied it as snugly as possible. The air coming in his screened windows was cool, so he pulled a dark blue sweatshirt over his T-shirt. Next he fashioned a dummy from some dirty clothes and lumped his blankets over the top of it. He glanced at his watch: ten-thirty. He turned off his light and lay stiffly next to the dummy on his bed. After a while, Shere Khan came in through the partially open door, scrambled up, and picked his way across the piled-up blankets. He settled next to Brendan's face, purring softly. "Hey, kitty," Brendan whispered. "You'll have to be content with a fake head tonight." Khan purred louder.

The full moon had risen and now cast enough light into the room for Brendan to see vague, shadowy shapes of furniture. He wished Nick were in a bed beside his. In the thin light, his mirror looked murky, and from where he lay, he couldn't see his reflection.

He counted his breaths. Inhale . . . one. Exhale . . . two. Or should inhale and exhale count as just one? Is counting breaths like counting sheep? Will it make me go to sleep? he wondered. He imagined everyone falling asleep and having Old Ph. wake him up in the morning, waving a laundry basket, demanding that he get all those dirty clothes out of his bed.

Boredom conflicted with anticipation. Brendan started to toss and turn, but space was limited. Hurry up! He directed the thought toward Mrs. Peterman. He looked at his watch. Nearly eleven o'clock. Now if she just decided to skip the news . . .

Chapter Fifteen

Finally, Brendan heard Old Ph. on the stairs, scuffling as if she couldn't quite find the right place to put her feet. He heard her mutter something about "crazy steps." She took a long time in the bathroom, but after she went into Mom's room, she shut the door with a thump, and that was it. No checking. No tucking them in for the night.

Brendan peered at his watch. Fifteen slow minutes went by. Then he heard three taps on his door. He leaped up, took just a moment to move Shere Khan closer to the dummy's head, and then opened the door wide for Nick and Ami.

"I thought she'd never go to bed," whispered Ami. She turned on her flashlight but kept her hand over it to cut down on the glare. Brendan looked away from the eerie sight of her fingers turned red and skeletal. "Come on," Ami continued impatiently. "You go first, Nick."

Nick was wearing clothing identical to Brendan's—jeans and a dark sweatshirt. As soon as he was through the window, Ami said, "Here, take the stuff." She shoved the three sleeping bags out, and they rolled down the roof. Nick helped them over the edge.

An inquisitive yelp followed the thuds of the landing sleeping bags. "Jeez, Brendan, why'd you leave Shag tied outside?" Nick asked.

"Remember at supper? Old Ph. said she didn't want the dog inside. Said she's allergic or something."

"Sh!" Ami hissed.

When Nick disappeared into the tree branches, Ami crawled out the window. Brendan noticed that she had her backpack and was dressed in her Maid Amelia outfit. The colors of the bright scarf looked deep and rich in the moonlight. He took a quick breath before following her.

As he climbed out onto the roof, he felt that he'd stepped over a boundary into a new place. Even the air was different—surprisingly chilly—and he felt the film of sweat on his face turn cold. Shag's excited whines added to the sense of adventure. He could hear Ami shushing the dog while she climbed down the tree.

The roof was covered with shingles, and Brendan felt their gritty texture crunching slightly beneath his sneakers. He got to the branch, grabbed it, and swung into the leaves. He felt with his hands—thought with them—as he climbed down, from limb to limb along the cool, rough-barked trunk. The leaves had a distinct odor that he had never noticed before. It's like I'm blind, he thought, and my other senses are taking over.

"Brendan, you put Shag in the house," Ami ordered in a hoarse whisper when he reached the ground. "If we leave her out here, she's bound to bark. Inside, she should be quiet."

Shag leaped up on him, licking his arms and hands in an ecstatic greeting. He unlatched her chain and dragged her by the collar up the back steps. He pried open the screen door slowly to prevent a telltale squeal. But when he pushed against the solid door, it wouldn't budge. Stuck, he thought, and shoved hard with one shoulder. Then he realized that Mrs. Peterman had locked it. He groaned as he pulled Shag back down the steps.

"You have a piece of rope?" he asked. "We'll have to take Shag along. Old Ph. has locked us out."

"Rats," muttered Ami. "Unhook her chain and use that."

"Too long. 'Sides, it'd rip my hands to shreds," said Brendan. "You don't have a rope?"

Nick said, "Yeah, you must have something with you to lead the unicorn home."

"No, I don't. And if I did, I wouldn't use it on a *dog*." Ami's voice rose in anger.

"Quiet! You wanna wake Peterman?" asked Nick.

"Forget it," whispered Brendan. "I'll just hang onto her for now and tie my socks together to make a leash later. Let's get going if we're going to go." He felt the adventure deteriorating, as if the magic of the night were being dissolved by all the bickering.

But as soon as they started across the meadow with its tall grass bending, like parting water, he felt the excitement returning. Shag trotted next to him, her nose high as she sniffed the night air. *The dwarf's trusty hound followed the scent of the ogre,* Brendan thought. When they reached the woods, Brendan stared hard into the dense vegetation, half expecting to see the strange shadow again. They were surrounded by darkness, and as they stepped into the depth of the woods with nothing but a feeble flashlight beam to follow, he thought anything might happen. His grip on Shag's collar was tight, but she kept straining against it, and his arm was already beginning to ache.

"Wait. I've gotta make a leash now, or my arm's gonna fall off." They stopped, and Nick held Shag while Brendan stripped off his socks and tied them together in the beam from the flashlight.

Navigating the steppingstones in the dark wasn't easy. Especially with Shag bounding along next to Brendan, splashing and tugging on the short expanse of sock leash. But they managed to reach Swallow Hole without anyone falling in.

The water was glazed with moonlight and speckled with dark shadows. It looked opaque, like shimmering mercury. *Deadly* was the word that leaped into Brendan's mind. They skirted its perimeter cautiously.

The climb up along the tributary was the hardest part. Shag kept lunging ahead on the wrong side of saplings, stretching the socks and Brendan's arm. He had to stop and pull her back around each time. No matter where Ami shone the flashlight beam, it wasn't where Brendan needed it. He fell twice, and one knee was throbbing by the time they reached the side of the old barn.

They fought their way through the brush and weeds and emerged into a clearing. Brendan blinked when he saw the house where the ogre lived, sitting quiet and dark up the slope from the barn. His stomach clenched, but Ami was already going through a weather-beaten barn door that swung open on dramatically creaky hinges.

"We dwarves and Maid Amelia enter the labyrinth through the west gate," whispered Nick.

"Our faithful canine guardian pricks her ears to alert us to hidden dangers. She knows that the ogre is near," added Brendan. In fact, Shag's ears were pressed flat against her head as she resisted going into the barn, place of her former captivity. He had to drag her inside. Ami was swooping the light around, searching for a good spot to camp.

The ground floor of the barn was crammed with dusty furniture and machines. There were a few open spots and a narrow path through the jumble to a ladder that was built into a partition. The ladder led to the hayloft. "We'll sleep there," Ami said, pointing.

"I can't carry Shag up a ladder," said Brendan. "And she sure can't climb it either."

"Maybe you can just stay down here with her until it's your watch," suggested Ami.

"Watch? You mean like staying awake alone and looking out at the empty dark?" asked Nick.

"Precisely, Dwarf Wimper," said Maid Amelia. Brendan could hear the grin in her voice.

"Toss me a bale," he said as Ami and Nick climbed the ladder. "I'll make a nest for Shag here on the floor.

Then maybe she'll settle down so I can come up with you guys."

Ami persisted in hogging the flashlight, and Brendan had to keep begging her to direct the beam down from the loft to help him see. He used the twine off the bale to make a better leash for Shag and tied her to a heavy piece of old farm machinery. When Shag saw the bed of hay he'd made, she turned around and around, then sank gratefully down.

Brendan sat next to her for a few minutes, rubbing behind her ears, feeling her hot breath and tickling fur. Then he got up carefully and fumbled his way to the ladder and climbed it. Shag whined only once, but when he told her to stay, she was reassured that they were not going to leave her there alone.

In the loft, Brendan opened his sleeping bag, took off his sneakers, and crawled inside. The familiar camp-fire odors mixed with the scent of hay, like fresh-cut grass. For just a moment, he forgot everything and felt truly safe.

Chapter Sixteen

Ami set up the watch schedule: Nick, herself, Brendan. She claimed that Nick was the hardest to waken, so he had to have first shift. Nick stationed himself next to an opening in the side of the barn where a section of a board had broken off. His head, a dark blob that moved and sighed, was silhouetted against the sky. Brendan sighed, too. The stiff hay refused to mold to his body. He wished Shag could be up here with them and sleep next to him. He tossed and squirmed, and soon his sleeping bag had gotten twisted, and no amount of kicking helped.

"What's with you?" asked Nick. "You got a bug in there?"

"Probably," muttered Brendan. Maybe a spider had decided to make a nest at the foot of his sleeping bag. The thought sent him scurrying out. He shook the bag and spread it on the hay as neatly as he could in the dark. Then he crept around on top of it.

"What are you doing?" asked Ami groggily.

"Pest control. Primitive method of extermination," said Brendan, and Nick laughed.

Brendan wriggled back inside the sleeping bag. He stared upward at the numerous holes in the roof. There was no sign of stars, but faint paths of moonlight filtered through to make milky pools on the hay. He sat up and adjusted his sleeping bag one more time. When he lay down again, his eyelids felt heavy.

The dream began abruptly—a vivid image in sharp focus. His father was standing on the porch of their new home. There was a silvery light shining on him so that everything about him was in clear detail, from his tousled, bleached straw-yellow hair to the untied lace on his left sneaker. The light was moonlight, of that Brendan was certain. He had a sense of being there, too. He knew that he wanted to ask Dad a question, but he couldn't make a sound. Yet Dad turned slowly toward him and nodded, as if in answer. Then suddenly he laughed, the deep chuckle that Brendan found so familiar but which, even in his dream, he realized he'd almost forgotten. His father looked tall and strong. The skin at the corners of his eyes was crinkled from smiling. His eyes were made up of chips of color, like mosaics. Like miniature pieces of a clear blue sky. Dad nodded again.

Brendan woke up with Ami shaking his arm back and forth. He thought he'd just gone to sleep and was about to grumble, when he recalled the dream. He sat up quickly to show he didn't need further prodding. He wanted to keep his mind focused. He refused to let go of the dream, waiting for it to cross over and become part of his wakeful memory. Take a deep breath and let it out slowly . . . slowly. Yes, I still remember it, he thought. I still remember Dad.

Brendan smiled with satisfaction, then smiled more broadly, realizing that it was silly, here in the dark where no one could even see his expression. Usually, his dreams vanished as soon as he woke up, leaving only the vaguest memories. But he would not forget this dream. He could return to it, see Dad again, whole and well. Laughing. Mosaic eyes smiling.

"It's your turn to stand watch," said Ami. There was a soft, scraping sound as she lit a match. Ami held it to a candlewick and then lifted the flickering flame above her head. She blew out the match. The candle-light wavered; shadows danced on her face.

"God, Ami. Put that out!" Brendan felt real alarm. "You're going to burn us all up!"

"Light is power," she whispered, but the flame moved uncertainly downward.

"Whatever. But put it out. *The moon is full with magic.* Right? We don't need candles!"

Brendan crawled out of his sleeping bag and stood in front of Ami, holding his breath until she blew out the candle. Then he glanced around in the darkness, searching for sparks. He saw none. "O.K. Let me have the matches. I might need them." He sensed Ami's hesitation. "Come on!" he said impatiently. "You've got the flashlight. It's only fair to share the light sources." With a sigh, she moved toward him and pressed the packet of matches into his hand. "Anything left to eat?" Brendan asked, deliberately casual, feeling sweat pooling in his armpits despite the chill in the air.

"Yeah. Some Jell-O mix and a couple of apples. Nick really pigged out on his watch. And he spilled our juice." Ami sounded normal now.

"Cute." Brendan could hear his brother's steady breathing. Was Nick dreaming? The same dream he had just had?

"What time is it?"

"It's a little after three," answered Ami.

Brendan folded his arms across his chest, shivering suddenly. Then he grabbed his sleeping bag and wrapped it around his whole body. He waddled to the opening; the hay hurt the soles of his feet, but he didn't want to bother looking for his shoes. He peered outside. There were no lights in any of the windows in the old house.

Brendan patted the air with one hand until he located a bale to sit on. From this angle, he couldn't see around the corner of the barn to the side field where a unicorn would most likely hang out. I must still be half asleep, he thought. Now *I'm* looking for the unicorn. He blew on his cold fingers. Soon his eyes began to ache from staring at nothing. He pulled his sleeping bag more snugly around himself.

"Ami?" His voice was small in the dark space of the barn. No answer. He doubted that she was asleep already. She was probably ignoring him just to be annoying. He decided not to give her the satisfaction of calling again. Brendan stifled a yawn.

"What?" Ami's delayed reply startled him, and his

mind fumbled for a moment, trying to recall what he'd wanted to ask her.

"You ever dream?"

"Yeah. Everybody dreams," said Ami. "I've read some stuff about sleeping and dreaming. You dream during REM sleep. That stands for 'rapid eye movement.' Really scientific, huh?" She snorted, and Brendan could hear the hay rustling as she moved.

"Shag dreams," he said. "I've seen her moving her legs like she's running."

"Right. RLM."

Brendan grinned and said, "Rapid leg movement." Then he added, "I don't dream very often. Least not that I remember. Do you remember your dreams?"

"Sometimes."

Brendan took a deep breath. In a way, he was hesitant to go on, yet he knew that he now had Ami's attention, that she was there behind him lying tensely, waiting for him to finish. He felt a connection with her that he hadn't sensed in a long time. Maybe because Nick was asleep, and Mom was miles and miles away.

"Have you," Brendan began slowly, "ever dreamed about Dad? Like . . . he was alive again?"

"No." Ami's answer came quickly. Then she said in a whisper, "Not that I remember, anyhow."

"I just did. I dreamed he was here."

"Here?"

"I mean on the farm." Brendan rubbed his itchy nose. "Our farm, not this one. Actually, he was standing on the porch of our house. But somehow, I knew, even in the dream, that he wasn't alive again. But he was there, clear as anything . . . just . . . well . . . standing there and laughing. And his eyes looked like . . . like his eyes. You know? Like real."

Ami was quiet. He turned toward her. Although he stared hard into the thick blackness, he could not see her. Finally, he heard her voice, so soft it was lost in the whisper of the hay as he shifted his weight.

"What?" Brendan asked. He wasn't sure she'd repeat whatever she had said. He sensed that she was slipping away from him, retreating like some small animal back into its burrow.

But when she answered, her voice was firm. "Real."

He wriggled his toes again, feeling uneasy. "Yeah," he said reluctantly.

"So," Ami said, "what's real? What about *death*, Brendan. Is that *real?*"

Maybe it'd been a mistake, sharing his dream with Ami. But he couldn't quit now. "Sure. Death's real. Everybody dies. Everything . . ."

"Do you ever think about dying?" Ami's voice was louder now and held a challenge. "I mean *you*, yourself dying?"

Brendan shrugged, then realized she couldn't see him. "No, not much, I guess." He suddenly had a nearly irresistible urge to wake Nick. He needed him.

"You know something? Maybe the unicorns died," said Ami.

"I guess they could be extinct," Brendan said hesitantly. He felt unsure, stepping into Ami's territory. It was like walking on the rocks in the stream. Which ones would be slippery? Where should he step next? "If they are extinct," he said carefully, "then there aren't any more alive, right? And that's what we've been telling you all along, Ami. I mean, isn't believing in a unicorn like . . . sort of like believing in Santa Claus?"

"No. This is different," Ami said intensely. "Mythical creatures aren't commercial fabrications. Unicorns were in tapestries, represented in art for thousands of years. So they must have been real. Maybe there were only a few. Maybe they were very rare. Like an endangered species."

"But if they're extinct . . ." Brendan let his voice trail off.

"I didn't say they were *extinct*. Just that most of them might have died. There could still be some. Just a few. Just . . . just enough. Maybe just one." Her voice was hoarse. Then he heard her moving restlessly before she added, "There's a unicorn out there. I *know* it. It's real."

"Why?" Brendan whispered. "Why does it have to be *real*?" He knew he was asking himself this question, too.

"I think . . ." Ami's voice sounded pinched, as if her throat were tight with tears. "I think it's got to be real, because if it's real, then I can believe in other things."

Brendan imagined how Nick would have replied. "Like Santa Claus's reindeer, Ami? So you want to believe in unicorns *and* in deer that fly?" But Brendan kept quiet.

Nick muttered something in his sleep and then asked thickly, "What time is it?"

"Around three-thirty," Ami answered. "It's Brendan's watch. Go back to sleep."

Brendan was tempted to say, *No, don't! Stay awake*

143

so we can do this together. But he heard the soft sounds of protesting hay and then Nick's steady breathing.

"Ami?" Brendan felt a strange compulsion to keep the conversation going.

"Huh?"

"What . . . what do you think happens after somebody dies?" he asked.

"Well, Granny Rodrick says they go to heaven where the streets are paved with gold."

Brendan could picture Dad shaking his head at the extravagance. "I wasn't asking about what *Granny* believes. You. What do *you* think?"

"I don't know. But then, I don't see how anyone can know. That's it. No one knows for sure. Not even the smartest or the most religious person really knows. Nobody. Except God, maybe."

"O.K., O.K., I get your point," said Brendan.

"After death there could be just about anything." Ami was whispering again.

"Or nothing," Brendan countered. Yet he could not imagine nothing.

"Now, see, if we catch the unicorn, then it's got to be real, right?" Ami was still on the unicorn track.

"I guess so," said Brendan, but he was trying to make his mind comprehend nothingness.

Ami's voice was suddenly very distinct, as if she'd moved closer. "Catching the unicorn would prove that other stuff can be real, too. Like, for instance, life after death. You see, Brendan?"

"Not really. It's too dark," he said lightly but added quickly, "Yeah, I guess I do get it. Sort of."

144

And it was clear to him suddenly. He understood. Ami wanted to prove to herself that the unicorn was real. That way she could believe that their father was not gone. That he was still "real" somewhere. Is that such a crazy idea? he wondered. Maybe not.

"Brendan," Ami said softly, "do you know what I said to him? I mean, the very last words I said to Dad? That morning?"

"No, Ami, don't . . ." He didn't want her to talk about that unseasonably warm day in early December when their father had left and never come back.

"It was just as I was leaving for school. He told me to pick up some stuff I'd left lying around from a school project I was working on. I'd made a big mess. 'Pick it up, please,' he said, 'we're all part of this family, even teenagers.' He was sort of joking about it. But I got mad. Real mad. And I ran out the door and screamed, 'I hate you!'"

"Ami . . ."

"I didn't really mean it. But I . . . I never got to say I was sorry. Or anything. . . ." Her last words were raspy, and she began to cry.

"Oh, Ami . . ." Brendan's voice failed him. He listened to his sister sniffling as he stared out through the slit in the barn, keeping watch. But he was remembering that day. A car had bumped, just bumped, their dad's bicycle, and he'd been knocked over in front of the wheels of an oncoming truck. It happened in the morning, shortly before the temperature dropped and the drizzle turned to snow. "Died instantly," the doctors kept saying, and everyone acted as if that were some sort of blessing. Brendan knew it was good Dad hadn't suffered, but so much was left unfinished, unsaid, undone.

Now he wanted to comfort Ami, but no words came to mind. His thoughts drifted back to his dream. What had he been trying to ask Dad? Do you still love us? Will I always remember you? Do you forgive Ami? Whatever the question, Dad had nodded, so the answer was yes.

Chapter Seventeen

Wide awake now, Brendan kept watch. Time seemed suspended—like the moon. Some wild animal scurried in a corner of the barn. Shag whined, and Brendan could hear her moving off her bed of hay, her toenails scratching the wooden floor as she strained against her collar. Above his head, a pigeon's feet made a faint, sandpapery sound on a beam.

Ami had stopped sniffing back tears, and Brendan thought she'd gone to sleep. He could hear both her and Nick's soft breathing. He kept his eyes focused on the moonlit view outside. Driveway, house, woods. Driveway, house, woods. Slowly and methodically, he moved his eyes, letting them rest on each element for several seconds. Everything was motionless, as if held in some sort of spell. Driveway, house, woods.

He let his gaze linger for a few moments on the house. In the light of the moon, it appeared as old and dilapidated as the barn. How could somebody live in a place like that? He glanced again toward the driveway.

What was that?

A shadowy shape was moving, coming into his line

of vision from the right. He rubbed his eyes, blinked, looked again. The shape had reached the driveway.

Shag's first bark was like the crack of a gun. It sent a shock wave through his body. The creature out there, in the moonlight, stopped. Its tail went up as it sprinted across the driveway. Brendan heard the splatter of gravel thrown from galloping hooves.

Shag was barking wildly now. The noise reverberated in the barn, and Brendan sensed Nick and Ami moving behind him. But his attention was riveted to the scene outside. It was as if a still photograph had suddenly come to life. *The moon is full with magic.*

A moment later, the front door of the house swung open violently and crashed against the wall. The ogre let loose a stream of curses. His dark figure emerged from the shadows and came stumbling down the slope toward the driveway. One arm was raised, and Brendan could make out the shape of a shotgun. He could hear shouts as the figure chased after the dark creature that twirled in the moonlight, tail flying. "Get back, you troublemaker!" the ogre yelled. "Get yourself back where you belong!" Shag's barks turned to whines.

"What is it?" Ami's voice was frantic.

Without even thinking, Brendan answered, "The unicorn!"

Ami bumped against Brendan, shoving him aside to see. "Oh no! My God, he's going to kill it!" Ami turned on the flashlight and dashed across the loft. The beam of light bounced crazily around the barn and then abruptly disappeared as she climbed over the edge and descended the ladder.

"Ami, wait!" Brendan called. He began to stumble around, tripping over his bundled sleeping bag in the dark. Where were his stupid shoes?

"Jeez, Ami!" Nick yelled. "What are you doing?"

The blast of the shotgun yanked Brendan back to the viewing hole. He squinted, trying to see what was happening. The ogre was still yelling and waving his gun.

"Stop! Don't! Don't shoot!" Ami was screaming now. Brendan heard her blundering through the debris on the ground level of the barn. Shag gave an anxious yelp. The sound of the creaky door grated against Brendan's ears.

"We've got to stop her!" Nick sounded desperate. "She'll get herself killed!"

"I can't find my sneakers!" Brendan cried. With each step, stiff hay pricked the bare soles of his feet.

"Where's the ladder? Wait, here it is. Hurry up, Brendan!"

A scraping sound, a cry from Nick, and then a dull thud made Brendan hold his breath.

"Ow! I think I broke my ankle!" Nick cried.

From outside came more voices—the ogre and Maid Amelia, yelling at each other incoherently.

"Brendan! Where are you?" Nick's voice was strained with pain and fear.

"I'm coming!" His fingers touched one shoe, and he grabbed it like a lifeline.

"I'll stop her," Nick said grimly.

Brendan heard Nick scuffling across the floor. Then the big door protested on its hinges, and he knew that he was alone in the cavelike dark of the barn.

From outside he heard, "Don't move!" The ogre sounded wild. Brendan jammed his bare foot into his sneaker. His fingers scrabbled across the hay, searching for its mate.

"Wait! That's my sister!" Nick said.

"Get over here!" the ogre shrieked. "Both of you! Get in the house. Now! Before I give you a taste of this buckshot."

Brendan located his other sneaker and put it on. His ears were tuned to the noises outside, but the voices were low now, and he couldn't understand what was being said.

He crept across the hay, feeling his way to the edge of the loft; then he searched for the ladder, groping right and left until his hands bumped into the wood upright. He slid one foot down carefully until he located the first rung. The pit of his stomach felt empty, like the air beyond the loft.

With a deep breath, he swung out over the edge. He concentrated his thoughts on the ladder. Problem with this stupid thing . . . straight up and down, no slant to it at all. He climbed slowly, placing his feet just right so he wouldn't slip off. His eyes had adjusted to the dark, allowing him to see the lighter, moon-drenched sky through the openings in the roof and the cracks in the sides of the barn. But within the barn, the night was as thick as mud. He understood now, all too well, how black was the absence of color. His eyes hurt from trying to see.

The floor came as a surprise. For a moment, he stood there, leaning against the ladder, feeling the solid planks beneath his feet.

Brendan tried to slow and steady his breathing. But there was a tremor somewhere inside that sent tiny vibrations all the way out to the tips of his fingers. He felt prickly all over, and he knew it wasn't because of the hay dust.

Once a few years ago, he and Nick had been held up by some teenagers on their way home from school. Then he'd had the same trembling inside, the same thudding heart that felt like some wild thing trying to batter its way out of his chest. But this was worse. Now he was alone.

Brendan pushed himself away from the ladder. He moved like a blind person without a cane, feeling and fumbling his way around the machines and other junk. Shag brushed her nose against his hand as he passed her. "Sorry, girl," he whispered. "You can't come with me. Not yet."

He remembered the terrible squeak of the hinges and opened the door cautiously and only far enough to peek outside. The moonlight looked amazingly bright, but he could see no sign of Ami, Nick, or the ogre. He could hear nothing except the chirping of crickets and the drone of other nocturnal insects. Glancing up at the sky, he saw a bat soundlessly swoop past.

If he slipped out and ran, he could get away without the ogre seeing him. He could run for home and help. Brendan hesitated, uncertainty making him feel slow-witted. Then, in the still night air, he heard a crash from inside the house. Shag whimpered.

"Wait here," he whispered to her and then stepped out into the moonlight.

He went up the driveway with his heart still hammering. No light shone from the house. He moved to the left, skirting the rickety-looking porch and front door. Maybe he could peer through a window and find out what was going on. The sweat on the back of his neck felt like the grasp of icy fingers.

As he got closer to the front of the house, he stared at the window. His heart lurched at the sight of Nick approaching. It took only a fraction of a second for him to realize he was seeing a blurry reflection of his own pale face. Where's Nick? he thought. I want Nick! Brendan averted his eyes and took a deep breath.

He went closer and peered in through the dirty glass. Nothing. He couldn't see inside at all. Just his reflected image stared eerily back at him. Brendan stood as still as a tree stump and listened, but he could hear no voices or sounds from the interior of the house.

I've got three choices, he thought. Three. Run home for help. Sneak inside. Knock on the door. He decided on number three. It was the fastest and most direct approach. Without giving himself time to change his mind, he scurried up the two steps and across the narrow porch. He yanked open the screen door and pounded hard and heavy on the inner wooden one.

Brendan waited. He wished that he had x-ray vision or some special powers. Sometimes he and Nick speculated about whether they could communicate telepathically. Not very well, they'd decided. But they'd read about identical twins who always knew if the other was sick or injured. Brendan didn't want to think about Nick's being hurt or even . . . dead. He didn't want to think about anything.

Time held its breath. But Brendan could not stop breathing, thinking . . . and remembering.

The day their father died, they'd been at school. Just before lunchtime, the temperature had gone down, and a gentle snowstorm swirled downy flakes outside the second-story window. Brendan had been hoping they'd get let out early, when the intercom crackled and the principal's voice, sounding tinny and far away, said, "Please send the Rodrick twins to the office." In the hallway, they clowned around, tossing a wad of paper off the wall until they turned the corner and saw the principal standing outside her office door. She started forward, then stopped; the distance between them abruptly seemed to lengthen. But even as they sensed that something was terribly wrong, they hadn't known, hadn't guessed. The principal's words had reverberated slightly in the emptiness. "Your mother'll be here soon. . . . I'm sorry, boys," she'd said.

That moment had been like this one, filled with dread. As if retreating from the memory, Brendan began inching away from the door. He moved down the steps and scurried backward on the rough path. He was just about to turn and dash for the woods when the door lurched open and the ogre—Old Mr. Johansson—shoved himself outside. He had a large, black flashlight in one hand and his shotgun in the other.

The beam of light caught Brendan full in the face,

blinding him and freezing him like a wild animal in headlights.

"Who the hell . . . ?" The man's voice faltered. The light trembled and skittered up and down Brendan's body. "You? How'd *you* get out here?"

He thinks I'm Nick! Brendan thought as he leaped aside and hurled himself toward the protection of some bushes. He expected to hear the blast of the gun, but instead there were just mutters of confusion from the ogre and the clap of the door closing behind him.

Brendan peered from his hiding place, trying to breathe steadily. The house was dark and quiet—like a sealed tomb.

Chapter
Eighteen

A worried yelp came from the barn.

Shag's calling me, Brendan thought. He turned and ran. This time he didn't bother to worry about the squeaking door. "We'll do this together," he told Shag as he untied the rope. She snuffled his fingers, then licked them appreciatively.

Dwarf Wimpet and his trusty hound skirt the prison, searching for a point of entry. But the imaginary story was inadequate for the emotions that made his mouth dry and his legs weak. He and Shag crossed the crunchy gravel and sneaked around the house, avoiding the front door. Shag lurched at the end of the makeshift leash. She was quiet, though, as if she understood the need for stealth.

Weeds and small trees grew close to the edges of the house, trying to reclaim it as part of the woods. At the back, a porch with a sagging roof sheltered a dark door that looked like a yawning mouth with no teeth. For a moment, Brendan hesitated, wondering if he'd made a mistake bringing the dog. How could he sneak into the house with Shag blundering along beside him or, more likely, in front of him? But she'd come this far quietly; maybe she'd be good. She'll protect me from the ogre, Brendan decided.

He didn't knock. Instead, he eased open the screen door and then gently, but firmly, pushed at the wooden one. He counted on it not being locked, and it wasn't. It opened as if used frequently. Brendan and Shag went inside, nearly stepping on each other's feet.

A feathery tickle crossed Brendan's face, and his mind screamed *spider!* before he realized that it was just a thread hanging down. He gave it a jerk without thinking, and a pale yellow bulb went on above his head. In the moment it took for his brain to realize that this had been a foolish move, he saw an entryway jammed with boxes and stacks of yellowed newspapers with a path through the middle leading to an open door. He yanked the string again and stood in the darkness, his heart thumping against his ribs. Sh . . . sh . . . his mind whispered.

Moving cautiously, he stepped forward, toward the door he'd seen. He groped with one hand, the other still wrapped in Shag's twine. He found the doorjamb and leaned against it, taking careful breaths. I need light, he thought, reaching into his pocket for the pack of matches he'd taken from Ami.

Without letting go of Shag, he lifted his hands. Quivering fingers and darkness made it hard to strike the match. But when it burst into flame, Brendan's eyes searched the room hungrily. There was no sign of the old man, or Nick and Ami. Bundles of newspapers made a solid barricade along one side of the dismal room. Cardboard boxes and ancient furniture filled the remaining available space. But again, there was a path leading to another doorway. He memorized the layout, blew out the match, then spat on his fingers and pinched it dead. This firetrap needed no excuse to burn.

He breathed shallowly, trying not to inhale the peculiar odor of neglect and decay. He and Shag threaded their way along the path. There was a frantic, scuttling, small-animal noise behind some newspapers. Shag whined anxiously, then all was quiet. Brendan swallowed.

The silence was like a presence, sneering at him. He longed to call out frantically, scream for his brother. But his fear held the words inside. What would that old man do? What had he already done to Nick and Ami? Brendan's fingers touched the next door. He eased it open. In the darkness, a short distance away, he could see a thread of light around a doorjamb. He lit another match and let it burn only for a few seconds, just long enough to set his course through the jumble of furniture and objects. He had time to see various items on the floor—an old telephone book, pieces of crumpled paper, greasy-looking throw rugs twisted into grotesque shapes that reminded him of dead animals.

As Brendan moved forward in the dark, he stumbled over a heap of something and flinched as a mouse scurried away. Shag jerked after it, and he yanked her back, holding her nose to keep her from barking. When he let go, she whined and licked his fingers. Together they managed to navigate the path, Shag pulling in front of him, straining against her collar. He could hear her sniffing, her nose telling her what his ears and eyes could not detect.

Brendan held his free hand out in front of his body until his fingers bumped into the door. He touched the rough wood tentatively as his lungs sucked in some of the room's foul air. Then, without waiting to get up courage, without allowing himself another thought, he yanked open the door.

The kitchen before him was large but dim. It took him a few moments to see, really see, the whole room. Again the walls were lined with debris and boxes, but a portion of the cluttered counter was bare and clean. There was a large table filling the space in the middle of the room, and sitting at one end, facing Brendan, was Old Man Johansson. His shotgun lay on the table in front of him amid the clutter. One hand rested on the stock. On either side of the table, sitting quietly, stiffly, with moon-pale faces, were Ami and Nick.

Brendan swallowed and stared, trying to understand what was happening. He tugged on Shag's leash, and for once, she sat down obediently beside him.

When the old man spoke, Brendan felt himself flinch. "Just come on in. Might as well. Thought I wouldn't hear you sneaking up on me, huh?"

Brendan gulped, but before he could say anything, Johansson went on in a querulous tone. "So! You're *twins!*" He rubbed his stubbled face with one dirt-grayed hand. "Sneaking around. Spying on me! Who the hell do you kids think you are, invading my property? Trespassers! I ought to shoot you!" His gnarled fingers tapped the gunstock.

Brendan dragged his gaze from the gun and saw Ami's eyes. They looked desperate, staring hard into his own as if she were trying to tell him something. Nick's expression was turned inward. The beaded sweat on his brow, the way he blinked and shifted his eyes away from Brendan's communicated his pain.

"We're sorry," Brendan said to the old man. An apology was the first thing that came into his mind, and it was the total truth.

Johansson snorted and shook his head. "Think you can sneak around, act like fools, and then just say 'sorry'? I should have you arrested. The whole lot of you!" He muttered under his breath, then went on loudly, "You could have got yourselves killed. You could have broken your necks climbing around in that old barn in the dark. Then what would happen? I'd get sued, is what. Some lawyer'd be up here, tramping around on my property, waving papers at me, telling me I had to tear down my barn because it's a hazard. Hah! The only hazard is idiot kids like you!"

"You're right," said Brendan. He wanted desperately to calm the old man.

"Of course, I'm right. Just like the pool. People blaming me when it's damn fool kids. Getting themselves killed. Fools." He seemed to be agreeing with himself. Almost talking to himself. His next words were spoken in a low, mumbling voice. "Can't leave a body alone. Just want to be left in peace. Always something going haywire."

"We'll leave," said Brendan. "We shouldn't be here. Just . . . let us go. My brother and sister and I—we'll get right out of here."

The man looked up at Brendan. "Between that crazy beast and you fool kids, can't get a wink of sleep." His words sounded like a tape on the wrong speed. Low and slow. "Get out of here." He lurched to his feet, grabbing his gun in the process. Fear leaped back into Brendan's throat, but Johansson simply propped the shotgun against a box near the sink. He turned his back on the children and began to fill a rusty kettle with water.

Brendan looked at Nick. "You O.K.?"

Nick shook his head, glancing fearfully toward the old man's back. Then he whispered, "My foot, my ankle's bad. Hurts. Don't think I can walk."

Brendan turned his attention to Ami, whose skin reminded him of the color of chewed gum. Before he could say anything to her, Johansson said, "I need some tea." The old man's hands trembled as he set the kettle on the gas flame. Then he turned and stood next to his place at the table. His gaze wandered around the room and suddenly fastened on Shag. "That dog! That's *my* dog!" He leaned forward across the table. His jaw jutted out menacingly.

Shag was still sitting; now she leaned hard against Brendan's leg. Her tail thumped the floor apologetically. Some protection! Brendan thought. Clearing his throat, he said as firmly as he could, "She's our dog. You found her when she got lost, and you kept her for a while. Thank you."

"What? What's that you're saying? *Your* dog?"

Brendan nodded. "Actually, she belongs to our mom mostly. Shag was a present to my mom from our dad.

But our dad's dead. He . . . he died in December. And our mom really missed our dog when she was lost. Thanks for taking care of her," Brendan finished hoarsely.

Johansson sank into his chair. He scrubbed his fingers through his hair, then rubbed his eyes. His voice was rough and barely audible when he said, "Yeah. She's no great watchdog anyhow."

A greasy-faced clock on the wall behind Ami's side of the table ticked loudly, as if chipping away at the silence. Brendan moved slowly toward his sister, who looked stiff with fear. Shag came with him, her tail thudding into the boxes that crowded in from the walls.

"You all right?" Brendan asked Ami, touching her shoulder.

She looked up at him and shrugged. Then, as if the old man weren't still there, sitting only a few feet away, she whispered, "I thought he was going to kill us both. But, Brendan, I realized . . . I realized that I didn't *want* to die." Her lower lip quivered, and she placed the back of one hand against it.

"Good," Brendan said in a normal tone of voice. He was afraid Old Man Johansson would think they were conspiring against him if they whispered. "I mean it, Ami. Nobody wants you to die."

Nick braced his hands on the tabletop and stood up slowly. He winced and sucked in his breath with a whistle. There was a bluish tinge around his mouth and in the hollows of his eyes.

"I don't think you're going to get very far," said Brendan as he peered under the table at Nick's ankle. It

161

was already beginning to swell above the top of his sneaker. "You need to go to the hospital. Now. Uh, Mr. Johansson, do you have a car?"

"No. A truck. But it won't start."

"Where's your phone?" asked Brendan.

"No phone."

Nick looked as if he were about to throw up on the table when Brendan said, "His ankle might be broken. He needs to see a doctor."

The old man shrugged. He reminded Brendan of Ami in a way. It was as if he were beginning to retreat from them into his own world. But then Johansson said wearily, "Lay him down. Put his foot up. Probably just sprained."

"Yeah, well, maybe so. But he still needs it looked at." Brendan glanced at Ami. She was sitting on her chair, but she'd pushed it back as if to keep from touching any of the jumbled items that littered the tabletop. Her eyes were lost in dark shadows.

Nick sagged back onto his chair and shoved several boxes of cereal out of the way so he could lay his head on the table. Brendan didn't see an extra chair to prop up his leg, and he didn't want to suggest that Nick lie down on some filthy couch.

"I'll go for help," Brendan said, making up his mind as he spoke. It was the only solution. They couldn't just sit here, waiting for morning, and then have Old Ph. discover they were gone, and then what, call the police? No, he'd have to go for help.

"I'll go, too," said Ami.

"No!" Nick's cry was frightened. "Don't . . . don't *both* leave me."

"O.K., I'll stay," Ami said almost gently. "And Shag, too."

"You have the flashlight?" Brendan asked.

"It got broken," Ami answered.

Brendan didn't even bother to ask for a flashlight from the old man, who was now rasping, "Fool kids," over and over under his breath.

But as Brendan started cautiously toward the front door, Johansson followed, seeming calmer. A toppled, broken floor lamp blocked their way, and the old man picked it up, muttering, "Clumsy brats." When they reached the door, he pointed and said to Brendan, "Go to the left side of the barn. You'll find a path of sorts. It'll take you to the little creek, and that'll take you to the pool, and to wherever you want to go."

Brendan nodded. "Thanks."

The full moon was lower in the sky now, but it still illuminated the open space between the house and the barn. The whole sky had begun to blush lighter while he'd been in the old house.

Following Johansson's directions, Brendan moved quickly around the barn. He jogged, feeling almost confident. Without warning, he ran into something that acted like a spring, jarring him backward. Barbed wire! Fortunately, his stomach had hit only one prong, but he cursed as he fingered the triangular tear in his sweatshirt.

Brendan peered along the single strand of wire. Despite the moonlight, he could barely see it—rusty and sagging to the ground in places. Carefully he crawled under it, relieved at finding relatively short grass on the other side. He sprang up and jogged, accelerating quickly to a steady run.

His feet thumped into the soft earth. The moon seemed to be following him as he ran, like a shining globe of light rolling down the dome of the sky. *The moon is full with magic.* He could see the woods ahead, just a little ways now. . . . He slowed and moved more cautiously, searching for another segment of the fence, something to separate this open area from the woods. But he found no wire, just a well-worn path that led him toward a wall of trees.

Brendan peered into the darkness. He had not expected the shadowy trees to be so dense. He moved carefully toward a spot where the darkness lacked substance. Yes, it was an opening into the woods. He became aware of the birds, their voices clamoring in a raucous, jumbled greeting to the new day.

Drops of moonlight lay like silver pennies on the trail before him. He walked quickly through the woods.

What's that?

A large, dark shape blocked his way. The shape moved, and Brendan jumped in surprise. Then there was a startled snort, and an animal rushed toward him.

Brendan squinted up and saw a bright shaft of light, then felt warm breath and heard pounding hooves. A mass of darkness swerved around him on the narrow path. Long, black strands of hair swept across his face, stinging his eyes and making him gasp in astonishment.

In his mind's eye—in an image as clear as his father had been in his dream—the creature was a black unicorn.

Chapter Nineteen

Brendan stared back toward the open, moonlit space where the unicorn had disappeared. The unicorn! He forgot about racing down the hill for help. His thoughts—his whole being—were focused on what he'd just seen.

An early morning chill clung here among the trees, and his sneakers soaked up the dew. Suddenly Brendan shivered violently and sniffed. His brain clicked back on. No, he decided. He would not go blundering after the unicorn. It was enough to have been close to it, to have felt the sweep of its power and the sting of its tail. To have seen the light of its single horn.

Or had he simply imagined it all?

Brendan turned away from that thought and plunged along the path until he stumbled into a rail fence. On the other side, the woods were thicker, but he kept moving, grabbing fistfuls of branches and trunks of saplings to pull himself forward through the undergrowth. Suddenly he was sliding, crashing down a steep embankment. He couldn't stop. He landed feetfirst in the tributary stream. The icy water drenched his already wet sneakers and soaked the bottoms of his jeans. But he hardly noticed.

He headed downstream. Slipping, stumbling, crawling in the water and over the rocks, he made his way down the side of the mountain until he could hear the murmur of the waterfall at Swallow Hole. He rushed toward the familiar sound. His toe jammed into a rock, and pain spiked up his foot.

"Ow!" Brendan fell forward. His head slammed into solid rock, and he rolled sideways, sputtering as the water splashed into his face. Now his sweatshirt was wet, too. He was acutely aware of being very cold. He dragged himself onto a rock and sat shaking with his teeth chattering.

His eye . . . something was blurring his vision. Brendan reached up to wipe it and felt sticky warmth. Blood! He explored his forehead with his fingers, found the cut, and held his hand over it to stop the bleeding. He got up slowly and moved forward again, only vaguely conscious of the warm liquid oozing out around his fingers.

When he reached Swallow Hole, it was shrouded in eerie mist. He hesitated a moment, thinking of the drowned boy. Another accident. He shuddered and moved carefully along the edge of the pool until he located the path. The rest of the way to the trailer court was easy. The ground was solid and smooth-packed, and the leaves on either side brushed his shoulders, whispering, guiding him through the trees.

The woods came to an end, and Brendan could see

the sky—a cool, deep blue with a tinge of pinkish gold over the hilltops in the east. And there was the moon, no longer a globe. Now it looked like a translucent disk floating low in the sky.

He blinked repeatedly, trying to keep his vision clear. Streetlights marked the roads in the trailer court, giving the illusion of a miniature city. Inside several of the homes, lights were on. People were already up, getting ready for work. One more routine day for them.

Brendan began to run. There was a trailer with red shutters. Next, the one with the purple ducks out front. The windows of Jonny's trailer were dark, but Brendan did not hesitate to climb the metal steps and knock hard on the door.

Panda began to bark wildly. Her toenails scratched on the inside of the door. "Shut up!" a muffled, sleepy voice admonished.

"Hey! Wake up!" Brendan shouted. "I need help!"

"Quiet, Panda." The barks subsided to an aggressive growl.

"Who is it?" asked Jonny.

"Me. Brendan. From up the road."

As the door opened, Panda's snarling face thrust forward at the bottom, and Jonny's surprised one peered out near the top. "Cripes! What happened to you?"

"I fell. Can I come in?"

Jonny dragged Panda back and opened the door, then ushered Brendan into the kitchen and sat him at the table. Panda's attitude changed now that he was inside. She bounced next to him, begging to be petted.

"You're a mess!" said Jonny. "Wish Mom was

home. She's at the hospital, working in emergency. From the looks of it, you'll probably be seeing her pretty soon. Bet you need a bunch of stitches. . . ." Jonny's voice trailed off as he turned to the sink. He ran water on a handful of paper towels, then handed the dripping mass to Brendan.

As Brendan pressed the wad against his head, Jonny went on. "Look at the time! It's not even five o'clock yet. What happened?"

Brendan stared at the bloody paper towel in his hand, then looked up into Jonny's confused eyes. "Where's your phone?" he asked.

Jonny pointed. "Who're you calling?"

Brendan shrugged, feeling suddenly and completely inadequate. He was on the verge of crying.

Sandy came into the kitchen, her round face still flushed with sleep, but her eyes sharp. "Why's he here? Which one is he?" she demanded. "Look, he's shivering!" She sounded concerned.

"Get him a blanket," Jonny instructed.

Brendan pressed his grimy palm against his forehead, then looked at it, seeing a fresh splotch of blood. His teeth began to chatter.

"Hey," said Jonny. "You gotta keep pressure on it. Not keep taking it off." He grabbed the plaid blanket that Sandy had retrieved and draped it around Brendan's shoulders. Sandy sat on a chair, and Jonny perched on the edge of another. "So what happened?"

Brendan pulled the blanket close and took a deep breath. "We . . . we were up at that old guy's place. Up on the mountain. And my brother's ankle's hurt pretty bad. He needs to get to the hospital. Maybe I need to call an ambulance."

"No, wait. Sandy, go wake Greg."

"Who's here?" Greg's deep voice came from the narrow hallway.

"Look at him!" Sandy patted Brendan's back in an awkward attempt to comfort him. Then she added, "He's all bloody and icky!"

Brendan's eyes were stinging, and the room was getting dimmer. He laid his head on the table, feeling the slight crunch of toast crumbs beneath his cheek.

The conversation floated around him, unfocused and seemingly irrelevant.

"Come on," said Greg. He was shaking Brendan's arm. "You look like you need a trip to the hospital, too. We'll go get your brother, and I'll take both of you to the emergency room."

"I'll call your mom," offered Jonny.

"No, she's in New York. I guess you'd better call the lady who's staying with us. She's not going to be happy." Brendan felt queasy just thinking about Old Ph., but Jonny told him not to worry, that he'd take care of explaining to her.

"What happened?" Sandy asked. "Did Crazy Man Johansson try to kill you? Did he kidnap you? Did you catch the unicorn?"

"No," said Brendan, but he could go no further with an explanation.

"Dang! I wanted to see the unicorn. Can we build another lure?"

"Quiet, Sandy. Leave him alone!" said Greg.

"I'm just trying to make him feel better," said Sandy, sounding hurt.

Brendan's toe was aching and his head throbbing, and the blood was still seeping through the fresh paper towels that Sandy had pressed into his hand a moment before. All of this made him feel strange—different. But there was something more. It was as if he himself had changed during the night.

But before he could begin to puzzle over this idea, Greg put his hand on Brendan's shoulder. "You O.K.? Dizzy? Sick to your stomach?"

"No." Brendan stood up, swayed, and felt Greg's steadying hands.

It was good to have someone taking over. Someone older and responsible who could drive and knew how to get to Johansson's place without him even having to give directions. Brendan realized that he couldn't have done that anyhow. The only way he knew to get there was through the woods. As they drove out of the still-sleeping trailer court, Brendan noticed that the mist in the hollows was dissipating. He stared out the window of Greg's car and watched the landscape changing and developing—coming into sharp focus as the day began.

Chapter Twenty

By the time they arrived at Johansson's place, the sky was bright and clear, illuminating the dilapidated buildings. Nothing looked sinister or mysterious. Shag barked a frantic greeting as Ami came out of the house with her. Brendan noticed that Ami's Maid Amelia outfit looked faded. One end of the scarf was ripped, and a long strand of thread trailed nearly to the ground. Old Man Johansson followed Ami, stumbling like some sleep-deprived homeless character, his face stubbled and his flannel shirt shiny with grease. His muddy galoshes flapped against his legs as he squinted up at Greg, shook his head, and said, "Fool kids." He looked nothing like an ogre.

Ami insisted she had to walk Shag home. "We can't take her to the hospital. And she'll go nuts if we put her back in the barn," she said. Brendan had no energy for an argument.

Inside, the house was still dim, windows shrouded in curtains or covered over with debris. Brendan was glad that Greg made no snide comments. With matter-of-fact calm, Greg helped Nick hop out of the old house to the car. He instructed both boys to sit in the back and fasten their seat belts.

"Don't worry," Greg said to Ami. "I'll take care of them. You sure you're O.K. now? I'd feel better if you'd come with us to the hospital."

"No, I've got to get back to our house. What if Mom calls? And that lady, Mrs. Peterman, will be frantic by now. You said your brother was going to call her, right?"

Greg nodded, and Ami said, almost too softly to be heard inside the car, even with the windows open, "Thanks, Greg."

But judging by Greg's smile as he climbed into the driver's seat, Brendan didn't think any thanks were necessary. Greg seemed quite pleased to be rescuing a damsel in distress, or, to be exact, the brothers of a damsel in distress.

The hospital was over thirty miles away, and when they arrived, they spent hours within the sprawling brick building. The boys finally were ushered into a large treatment room, where they could hear other people rasping and coughing behind flimsy barriers of cloth. Jonny's mother was there, still working night shift, but she left at seven-thirty to go home and check up on Jonny and Sandy. They waited and waited. Mrs. Peterman came to sign papers giving the hospital consent to fix them up. She was understandably upset, and Brendan had no clue how to explain. He tried to apologize, but his "sorry" sounded lame even to his own ears. Mrs. Peterman insisted that it was her responsibility to call Mom, and after she did that, she looked even more sour.

"She's starting home immediately," Mrs. Peterman reported. "She said I could go, but I don't feel right leaving you boys here in the hospital."

"I'll stay," Greg said politely. "And I'm sure my mom will make sure Ami's O.K."

Mrs. Peterman managed to smile and pat Brendan's arm before leaving.

Finally, Brendan's forehead was stitched, and he was invited to watch the doctor bandage Nick's ankle. It had been x-rayed and found to be badly sprained, not broken. Brendan was thankful to have Greg there, asking no questions, just sitting patiently, waiting to drive them home.

Later, back in their own living room, Brendan and Nick flopped on either end of the couch. One had his head bandaged, the other his foot. Both stared at the TV, but they weren't watching. They could hear Greg and Ami talking in low voices in the kitchen. Then Greg came in and gave them each a light punch on the shoulder. "You two take care of yourselves and that wild big sister of yours, O.K.?" He left, and they heard Ami climb the stairs. They were alone now, waiting for their mother to arrive home from New York and wishing they could change things, but knowing they couldn't.

At last they heard the familiar sound of the car motor and the crunch of gravel. Shag leaped up from the rug and dashed to the window to give a welcoming bark. In less than a minute, their mother walked in the front door and stood staring at them. Her arms hung at her sides, slack and empty as if she'd rushed home without even bothering to collect her purse. She looked smaller to Brendan, and he wondered if worrying had made her shrink.

"Oh, you guys!" She rushed toward them. Brendan stood up to hug her, thinking there was no point in having both him and Nick look incapacitated.

"Ouch! Watch the foot," said Nick when Mom leaned over to kiss him.

As Mom sank onto the couch, there were tears in her eyes. "Boys . . . I just don't know . . . Oh, Nick, it isn't broken, is it?"

"Nah."

"And how many stitches did you get, Brendan?"

"I don't remember."

"He's got amnesia," said Nick.

Brendan forced a laugh. "I'm fine. I'd never be lucky enough to forget you, bro'!"

"Honest, Mom, they did say he might have a slight concussion from his brain getting whacked around inside his skull."

"Thanks, Nick," said Mom with a rueful shake of her head. "That's just what I need to hear."

Footsteps sounded on the winding staircase. Then Ami came haltingly into the room, her blond hair still damp from a shower and her face looking as if she'd scrubbed it too hard. She was wearing a clean, white T-shirt and denim shorts.

"Hi, honey." Mom's voice was almost a whisper. She rose partway from where she was seated next to Nick.

Brendan noticed that Ami's eyes were rimmed in

red. She stopped and stood silently for a moment, her fists clenched at her sides. Then, as if with determination, she relaxed her fingers and dashed into her mother's arms. "Oh, Mom, I'm sorry. . . ." Ami's words were nearly smothered in the embrace.

Brendan glanced away. He knew that Ami was saying she was sorry for more than last night. Mom seemed to understand. "I know, honey," she murmured. "I know."

Brendan went over to the television and turned it off.

Mom patted the couch. "Come here. All of you. Sit." They sat and squeezed together. Shag snuffled over and tried to climb into Mom's lap. Since there was no space, the dog jammed her nose under Brendan's hand, and he scratched her head. Shere Khan sauntered into the room, eyed the crowd on the couch, and sat on the rug. He began to wash his paws.

"I'd just sat down for breakfast when Mrs. Peterman called and said, 'There's been an accident. . . .'" Mom's voice cracked.

"What did you have?" asked Nick. "For breakfast. I'm starving." He grabbed the crutches he'd gotten at the hospital and stood up on one foot.

"O.K., food first," said their mother, dabbing at her eyes with a tissue. Shere Khan trotted after them into the kitchen and scrabbled onto the counter, then arched his creaky back and mewed plaintively.

"Honest, we did feed him," said Brendan, but he spooned some canned food into a bowl and set it on the floor.

They all sat at the table, pouring two or three cereals together into their bowls. Ami looked up almost shyly. "Cereal stew," she said.

"Yeah." Nick nodded.

Dad's name for it.

"Now," their mother said, "I want to hear it. The whole story from the beginning."

Nick turned toward Ami and said, "Yeah, from the beginning."

The pinkness had left Ami's face so it reminded Brendan of the pale moon in the dawn sky. She glanced up from her bowl; their eyes met. He knew she didn't want them to tell about everything—her dive into Swallow Hole, her fantasy world, and the unicorn hunt that was the real reason they'd gone to the old barn. No, Ami didn't want anyone to tell it from the beginning.

"It all started," Brendan said quickly, "when Old Ph., I mean, Mrs. Peterman arrived. . . ."

"Hey," interjected Nick, but Brendan silenced him with a meaningful glance. Nick took the cue and continued without missing a beat. "Yeah, right. She was like a warden, Mom, really. And the only time we could escape was at night. So we decided to sleep in that old barn because we don't have a tent and our barn has too many spiders. We need a tent, Mom. You know, I saw one in a flier that came in the mail. Not a bad price either."

"Nick, shut up," said Mom mildly. "What exactly happened after you'd gotten to the barn?"

Bit by bit, the story was told, each of them adding threads until it was loosely stitched together. They did not mention the unicorn.

Mom lectured them for a good fifteen minutes, saying "that poor old man" more times than Brendan felt necessary. After all, Mr. Johansson didn't have to scream and threaten and wave his gun. But then, none of them talked about the gun, so their mother had no way of realizing that they'd been in real danger. The tale they'd created had a certain lightness that made it sound like an adventure, nothing more.

Later Brendan went up to his room and plopped on his bed and let his gaze wander. He felt as if he'd been gone a long time, and everything looked vaguely unfamiliar. Had the walls always been so purple? Where had that pile of dirty clothing come from?

He got up and shut his door. His reflection looked back at him from the dust-filmed mirror. He tugged at one corner of the awkward white bandage that nearly covered his right eye. Gingerly, he pried it up and peered beneath. The edges of the cut were still raw and held together with dark stitches that looked very much as if they were made of thread from Mom's wall-patch basket. It was like a fake scar, the kind little kids put on for Halloween. But it was not going to wash off. Even after the stitches came out, he'd have a scar that everyone would be able to see.

Do you know I'm me, not a clone or just a twin? Maybe that was the question he'd tried to ask Dad in his dream. In his mind, Brendan saw again his father's nod. He lowered the flap of the bandage back over the stitches. He no longer needed to look different from Nick. But now, finally, he did.

Chapter Twenty-One

"Brendan?" Ami's knock sounded tentative.

"Come on in," he said, patting the bandage down into place and opening his door to her.

"I have something to show you." Ami stood staring at him expectantly.

"What?" he asked, feeling self-conscious suddenly, wondering if she realized that he was marked for life.

But she said nothing about his bandage or scar. "It's outside. Will you come? Mom's lying down in her room, and I think Nick's fallen asleep on the couch."

Brendan shrugged. "Sure, O.K."

He had trouble keeping up with Ami. She was charged with energy, while he still felt tired and sore. His toe was tender, his head felt too big for his skull, and his left arm hurt from the tetanus shot he'd gotten in the emergency room.

The sunlight stung his eyes; he almost wished for moonlight. Ami went to the barn, and Brendan trailed behind. She entered through the small door and turned left toward a pen that was separate from the cow stanchions. Brendan followed.

A black horse lifted its head from a pile of grass on the floor and nickered.

"It's a mare," said Ami simply. "She's part Arabian."

Brendan blinked and stared. Not part unicorn? he thought stupidly. His aching head couldn't seem to comprehend what he was seeing. He took a step backward, but he couldn't tear his gaze away from the animal. A horse? He shook his head to clear it.

All along he and Nick had thought those animal tracks belonged to a horse. Yet he found adjusting to the reality of one as difficult as facing the light of the sun. He stepped forward and reached out his fingers to touch the mare's nose. It was warm. He took a deep breath, remembering. The nighttime shadow in the meadow, the beast on Mr. Johansson's driveway, and the large, dark creature he'd encountered in the woods had been this horse.

Brendan sighed, feeling a sense of loss. Then he asked in a low voice, "How'd you catch it?" He almost used the word *capture*.

Ami stroked the mare's head. "I didn't have to. Mr. Johansson gave her to me."

"What?" Brendan shook his head in disbelief.

"It's true! What do you think, I stole her or something?" Ami asked defensively.

"No, but . . . Why'd he give you a horse?"

"Actually, it's all because he's got a son. Johansson does."

"A son?"

"Yeah, a son," said Ami. "And he lives someplace near New York City. The mare was his daughter's.

179

Johansson's granddaughter's. But she got boy crazy and lost interest."

Brendan was amazed. The ogre was a grandfather!

When Ami stopped talking to rub her fingers along the animal's neck, Brendan said, "So? What's all that have to do with . . . this?" He hesitantly moved closer to the horse, who stared at him with huge, dark eyes. Then the mare snorted.

Brendan jumped, and Ami laughed before she said, "I guess Johansson's son didn't want to sell her right away, thought maybe his second kid would get interested in horses."

"What?" Brendan asked again. He was having trouble following Ami's story, especially with this animal blowing hot breath in his face.

"Just listen! I'm telling you what happened. See, it was like this. I was terrified of him, Mr. Johansson. Even while Nick and I were waiting for you to get help, I felt like a scared little kid. We just sat there, the whole time, while he slurped his tea and muttered. Then, when you guys—you and Greg—drove up, and we went outside, and I looked at Johansson . . . You know, in the sunlight? He looked like . . ."

"Just an old man," supplied Brendan. "Somebody's grandfather."

"Yeah. I mean, *before* he'd frightened the living daylights out of me. But after you left . . . after you guys drove down the hill, Shag started barking at this horse that was standing on the other side of a falling-down fence next to the barn. And then Johansson, he starts talking to me. He says, 'Let me tell you, a horse is

180

nothing but trouble.' Then he goes on about how his son dumped this one at his place last fall because he thought maybe his younger daughter would get interested in horses someday. Johansson says that his son didn't want to pay to board the horse in the city."

"I still don't get it. What's that have to do with *you* getting her?"

"Shut up and listen!" Ami said impatiently. "Johansson thinks horses are useless hay-burners. And his fences are worthless, and she kept getting out, running around in the woods."

"Yeah," said Brendan, thinking of shadows and hoofprints.

"So, anyhow, Johansson gets this letter from his son a couple of weeks ago. I guess that second daughter skipped the horsy stage and went right for boys. The letter says Johansson can sell the horse and keep the money for his trouble. You should have heard what Old Man Johansson had to say about *that* idea. 'What's he think I am, a horse trader?' See, he didn't want anyone coming to his place to look at the mare. Strangers coming on his property, tramping around . . .'"

"Trespassers."

"Right. And then he starts talking about how he'd have to rent a truck and trailer and hire somebody to take the beast—that's what he called her—to the sale barn. And how that'd cost him more than he'd get paid for her. So . . ." Ami paused as if for dramatic effect. "I had this brilliant idea. I said to him, 'Hey, you want to get rid of the horse? I'll take her off your hands, and you won't have to worry about her ever again.'"

"That's what you said?"

Ami shrugged and gave Brendan a brilliant smile. "Well, something like that. And Johansson sort of cackled and said how we deserved to have the horse 'cause she was a pain in the neck and so were we. So he gave her to me, along with a halter and lead rope."

"Just like that?"

"Yes! So I led her and Shag both home this morning. And I spent ages combing the burs out of her mane and tail while you guys were off getting stitched and bandaged. I've got to arrange for the vet to come out and give her shots and worm her."

"So, does Nick know about this?"

"No! Pay attention, Brendan! I told you that it all happened after you guys left for the hospital."

The mare thrust her nose toward Ami, who dug into her pocket and brought out a bruised apple—a leftover from the unicorn hunt. With a soft murmur, Ami held out her hand, the apple balanced on her palm. The mare took it from her with dainty lips, then bit into it with a loud crunch and munched efficiently.

Brendan watched. So this is how you tame a unicorn, he couldn't help thinking. Aloud he said, "Doesn't seem quite fair, you know? You got us into that mess, and now it's like you're getting a reward."

"Johansson thinks a horse is a punishment," Ami said lightly as she wiped her slobbered-on hand across her shorts. "I'll have to get the fences in good shape. She's used to escaping. And I plan to buy that hay in Johansson's barn and hire some farmer to move it down here so she'll have food for the winter. Horses have to eat at least twice a day. And I'll muck out her stall. Unless, of course, you and Nick want that job."

"No, thanks!"

Brendan watched as Ami slipped an old halter over the mare's head and opened the gate to the pen with one hand. She asked, "Mom won't mind, will she?"

"About the horse? No, she'll be happy. She's wanted you to want a horse ever since we got here. She's just been waiting for you to ask."

"I guess I didn't think I wanted one. Because . . . a horse isn't like a unicorn." Ami stared at Brendan and then said softly, "I thought we were safe in the unicorn world. I thought if I truly believed, then nothing bad could happen. But when the ogre, I mean Mr. Johansson, caught us, and I thought . . . I . . . we were going to be killed, it was like I got to the edge and then . . . then I wanted to come back."

Brendan nodded. It did seem as if Ami had come back, and he was glad.

"Before all that happened," Ami said, "I didn't want a horse. I wanted a unicorn." She shrugged. "Come on, Brendan, let's take her out in the front yard so she can do some grass trimming."

They left the barn. Brendan put one arm over the mare's back and walked next to her, trying to match her steps. Flies came out of nowhere to buzz and dip around her. She was so big. And real.

"You know something, Ami?" he asked quietly.

His sister stopped and turned to look at him. The mare dropped her head and began to eat. A faint odor of bruised grass blended with a warm, horsy smell.

Brendan swallowed. "I wanted a unicorn, too."

"You did?" Ami tilted her head slightly, and the light touched her eyes, accentuating the tiny bits of color. Mosaic eyes like Dad's.

"A unicorn would have been cool," he said, feeling suddenly embarrassed. But Ami smiled. She pulled the mare's head up and gently reached out to brush aside her long, thick forelock.

"Look, Brendan," she whispered.

He peered at the mare's forehead. In the center, normally hidden by her forelock, was an almost perfect circular white spot.

"They call that a star," Ami said, and he noticed a trace of her Maid Amelia voice. "But it's not. It's an indelible mark, a sign of where her horn once grew." She looked at him, her head tipped back, as if daring him to contradict her statement.

"Maybe you're right," said Brendan, remembering the shaft of light in the dark woods. "She could be a unicorn who lost her horn. Unicorns could be real."

"That's what I've been trying to tell you all summer." Ami's tone was bantering.

"So maybe they could exist somewhere, right?" Brendan said. "And people could live forever. I mean, somewhere."

"Yeah, maybe," she said wistfully.

The mare lifted her head higher and stared toward the house. Unexpectedly, she nickered, as if in greeting. Brendan looked at the porch, remembered his dream about Dad, and smiled. Just then Nick hobbled out onto the worn boards, and Mom followed.

Brendan sprinted toward them.

Ami yelled, "Hey, wait for me!" He glanced back. She was right behind him, her hair fanning out in golden ripples and the mare trotting in long, graceful strides beside her. *A fair maiden and her captured unicorn.*

No, Brendan thought, my sister and her horse.